The Turret

OTHER YEARLING BOOKS YOU WILL ENJOY:

The Rescuers, MARGERY SHARP

Miss Bianca, MARGERY SHARP

Ben and Me, ROBERT LAWSON

Mr. Revere and I, ROBERT LAWSON

The Great Cheese Conspiracy, JEAN VAN LEEUWEN

The Cricket in Times Square, GEORGE SELDEN

The Genie of Sutton Place, GEORGE SELDEN

The Secret of the Sachem's Tree, F. N. MONJO

The Cricket Winter, FELICE HOLMAN

The Adventures of Benjamin Pink, GARTH WILLAMS

YEARLING BOOKS are designed especially to entertain and enlighten young people. The finest available books for children have been selected under the direction of Charles F. Reasoner, Professor of Elementary Education, New York University.

For a complete listing of all Yearling titles,
write to Education Sales Department,
Dell Publishing Co., Inc.,
1 Dag Hammarskjold Plaza, New York, N.Y. 10017

With Illustrations By
Garth Williams

By Margery Sharp

THE
TURRET

A YEARLING BOOK

Published by
Dell Publishing Co., Inc.
1 Dag Hammarskjold Plaza
New York, New York 10017

Yearling ® TM 913705, Dell Publishing Co., Inc.
ISBN: 0-440-48630-0
Reprinted by arrangement with Little, Brown and Company.
Printed in the United States of America

Sixth Dell Printing— March 1980

MPC

Contents

1

Miss Bianca at Home

MISS BIANCA sat at her desk in her Porcelain Pagoda writing a letter of resignation to the Mouse Prisoners' Aid Society.

Everything in the boudoir was beautifully light, simple and elegant. The furniture was of cedarwood, so that it smelled as well as looked nice, and the few cushions on the chaise longue, silk stuffed with swansdown, were all of the same pale pink. — How different from the rough surroundings of the Moot-hall, from whose platform Miss Bianca, in her capacity as Madam Chairwoman, had directed, and if necessary quelled, so many a stormy meeting! How different too her own discreet private stationery — bearing just the address, the Porcelain Pagoda, in blue on pure white rice paper — from the thick official sheets headed M.P.A.S., or M.P.A.S.L.G. (Mouse Prisoners' Aid Society Ladies' Guild), with things like "Office of Madam Chairwoman" or "Sewers and Drainage Committee" typed below! The pen in Miss Bianca's hand felt light as a feather — which indeed it was: a wren's quill.

Nonetheless, before signing her name, Miss Bianca paused. She was as conscientious as she was beautiful; and though she had examined her motives with extreme strictness, like many another very conscientious person felt uneasily that anything she very much *wanted* to do was perhaps something she *shouldn't*. It was against every inclination that she had been drawn into public life at all: her Porcelain Pagoda stood in the schoolroom of an Embassy, she moved with enjoyment in the highest diplomatic circles, and in hours of leisure found even keener delight in the cultivation of a gift for verse. Nor was it an existence without duties; the Boy, the Ambassador's son, never learnt his lessons half so well without Miss Bianca sitting on his shoulder to help him concentrate on some hard sum of arithmetic, or to revive, by some appreciative exclamation, his flagging interest in a page of history; even the Boy's tutor admitted her good influence — just as the Boy's mother did, who always allowed him to take Miss Bianca with him in his pocket to such things as Military Reviews, or Charity Matinées, that go on for hours and hours . . .

Only these were such *pleasant* duties! — Miss Bianca's conscience pricked her again.

Then she recalled the many occasions of late when

public and private duty had actually conflicted. While she was away helping to rescue a prisoner from the Black Castle, the Boy pined until he couldn't get even a simple addition right. The rescue of a child captive from the clutches of the Diamond Duchess had made her nearly miss a big dinner for the French Ambassador. (*"Je n'ai jamais rien vu de plus joli!"* exclaimed the French Ambassador, as Miss Bianca stepped delicately between the wineglasses to make her bow to him — he little guessed that she'd just escaped the jaws of bloodhounds.) Such memories as these quietened her conscience at last: when Miss Bianca recalled her experiences at the Duchess's hunting lodge (peril of

bloodhounds) and in the Black Castle (peril of cats and jailers), she really felt she'd done enough.

"My constitution will stand no more!" thought Miss Bianca. "I should become a nervous wreck!"

Also she had a slim volume of verse to prepare for publication.

"One has a duty to one's readers too!" thought Miss Bianca.

She dipped her quill into the ink again, and signed.

At that moment, a bell tinkled at the gate of the pagoda's little surrounding pleasure ground. Miss Bianca smiled as she rose to answer it. She knew very well who would be there — the Secretary of the Mouse Prisoners' Aid Society in person: otherwise her dear old friend Bernard.

2

"I hope I don't disturb you?" said Bernard anxiously. — It was shortly after midnight, a very proper calling hour for mice; but he was always terribly afraid of seeming to intrude, at least upon Miss Bianca. (Upon members of the M.P.A.S. who hadn't paid their dues Bernard intruded as ruthlessly as a bailiff. It was partly what made him such a good Secretary. The other parts were his extreme reliability, and coolness of judgment, and lack of self-seeking.)

6

"Not at all," replied Miss Bianca. "I had just finished writing a letter . . ."

"*The* letter?" asked Bernard eagerly.

"I'm afraid so," said Miss Bianca. Of course she had let him know her intentions in advance; and indeed he had influenced the decision.

"I'm very glad to hear it!" exclaimed Bernard.

Unreasonably enough, Miss Bianca felt a trifle nettled.

"I'm told — possibly by flatterers — that I made rather a good Madam Chairwoman," said she.

"Of course you did," said Bernard warmly. "You made the best Madam Chairwoman our Society ever had — or any Society ever had anywhere." (There are branches of the Mouse Prisoners' Aid all over the world, because there are unfortunately prisons all over the world.) "But I can't help being glad you're giving it up, because it'll mean the end of your risking your life amongst cats and jailers and so forth. As you know, I was against it from the beginning: you're too beautiful," said Bernard simply, "to be *allowed* into deadly peril."

Very beautiful indeed looked Miss Bianca, as she smiled affectionately back at him. Through the schoolroom window the rays of a full moon frosted her ermine fur to argent; the fine silver chain about her neck gleamed like diamonds — but not less brightly than her eyes. Or rather, the light in Miss Bianca's eyes was softer; they were brown (very unusual in a white mouse) and fringed by long dark lashes which lent them a most wonderful, tender depth. Bernard swallowed.

"Of course the Society'll want to give you a Dinner," he said huskily.

Miss Bianca sighed. Mice are very fond of giving Dinners, there is nothing they like better than to see six matchboxes end-to-end spread with shrimp tails in aspic and deviled sardine bones; all they need is an excuse. Bernard knew this as well as Miss Bianca, so that her sigh didn't offend him.

"Oh, dear!" said Miss Bianca. "With speeches?"

"Naturally with speeches," said Bernard. "First me, then the President of the Ladies' Guild, then you. If we can keep any of the others off their feet, it'll be a miracle."

Miss Bianca sighed again. Moving in diplomatic circles as she did she was used to a rather high standard of after-dinner speaking: the prospect of having to sit through perhaps half-a-dozen predictable and pedestrian orations thoroughly dismayed her. Also it was August, a month in which the best after-dinner speech always seems much longer than usual . . .

"Couldn't they give me something a little *cooler?*"

suggested Miss Bianca. "A picnic, for instance? — However, do not let us meet boredom halfway, but rather enjoy this pleasant evening by taking a little stroll."

Bernard was only too willing; arm-in-arm they began to promenade the small but charming pleasure ground. It was where they had first met, beside the Venetian glass fountain: Bernard then but a shy young pantry mouse, almost too awkward to speak, to the famous Miss Bianca! Now he was stout and important, but it seemed to him as but yesterday. Miss Bianca hadn't changed at all. Her elegant little figure moved with the same easy grace, her weight on Bernard's arm was no more than a snowflake's; only as she looked at the pretty swings and seesaws upon which she had been used to disport herself, she smiled. She hadn't swung on a swing for months.

"Time passes, my dear Bernard!" said Miss Bianca softly. "I am ready indeed, to retire to private life! — I didn't so much mind the perils," she added, "it was the *society* one was forced into!"

"That Head Jailer in the Black Castle was the worst," recalled Bernard.

"No," said Miss Bianca thoughtfully, "I believe Mandrake was the worst." (Mandrake was the Diamond Duchess's steward.) "The Head Jailer's habits were of course deplorable — indeed, the memory quite nauseates me now, of all those cigar butts left strewn about! — but *he* was being cruel, or so he believed, to desperate criminals; *Mandrake* was cruel to a defenseless child, whom but one kindly look or word might have saved from despair . . ."

"It was you who saved her from despair," said Bernard soberly.

"I must admit that to know her now safe and happy is one of my greatest comforts," said Miss Bianca, "but *Mandrake* I shall ever hold in abhorrence."

"Can't we talk of something more pleasant?" suggested Bernard.

— He really meant, more romantic. But Miss Bianca, though by her smile she seemed to acquiesce, just asked him to turn the fountain on.

"In this moonlight, it should look quite beautiful," said she, "and you know I'm not strong enough myself!"

Actually even Bernard had to sit down, on the spring that controlled the water supply, to make it work. He did so now almost too energetically: the resultant jet of water drenched Miss Bianca to the skin. But she took the mishap with her usual debonair good breeding, and in fact it gave her a splendid new idea. As Bernard, red in the face, respectfully wiped her down with his handkerchief —

"Bernard!" exclaimed Miss Bianca. "Could not the Society give me a *water* picnic? How long must it be, since we had a water picnic?"

3

The reason why the mice hadn't had a water picnic for so long was because it was so difficult to arrange. Everyone knew where a proper water picnic took place — on the lily moat beneath a ruined turret standing in neglected parkland some miles outside the city boundaries. Very old grandparent-mice remembered going there in celebration of the tercentenary of Jean Fromage — the heroic French mouse who'd once rescued a French sailor boy from slavery in Constantinople: since when the trouble of arranging transport, and hiring boats, and finding babysitters, had left the lily moat unvisited. But upon such an occasion as the resignation of Miss Bianca, and under Bernard's enthusiastic leadership, all obstacles were surmounted.

A mouse domiciled in the files at the General Post Office reported an outgoing mail van (room for any number) leaving at ten A.M. and halting in its circuit to empty a letterbox at the parkland's very gate: a second, returning, emptied the letterbox again at six; really quite an ideal schedule. Bernard personally made the whole trip in advance, in case the timetables had been altered, and while on site concluded a deal for boats with a colony of water rats established on the lily moat's brink. As for babysitting, when the great fatigue entailed by such an excursion had been pointed out to them, also after Miss Bianca had signed a few photographs for distribution amongst absentees, a more than sufficient panel of grandmothers was mustered ready to stay at home and babysit.

2

The Lily Moat Picnic

IT WAS THE most successful picnic imaginable.

Punctual to the minute set forth the Post Office mail van: punctually, even early, while it still waited in the Post Office yard, had the Mouse Prisoners' Aid Society boarded it — hauling on hamper after hamper. All the elder ladies wore best hats, and the younger ones floral topknots; Miss Bianca's own elegant ears were protected by a most becoming light lace handkerchief tied under the chin. Bernard brought his mackintosh.

Off the van rolled, tooting its horn. — As it approached each mailbox it gave an extra toot, to show people their letters were really being collected, and this the mice enjoyed extremely. Indeed, such an *esprit de mail van* rapidly rose among them, they joined in with hip-hurrahs. A special three-times-three saluted the box at the park gate, before all scrambled down and made for the lily moat, where (thanks to Bernard) a score of handy vessels — skiffs, canoes and catamarans — were moored in readiness. As for the weather, it was quite perfect: not a ripple discommoded as upon waters azure as the sky one and all embarked.

The novel aquatic experience proved so delightful, hither and yon from lily leaf to lily leaf paddled or sailed the happy party all morning, ere landing on the largest leaf of all to unpack lunch. The Ladies' Guild, who provided it, had excelled themselves: there was everything mice like best — that is, cold; they couldn't have deviled sardine bones or toasted cheese, but no other delicacy lacked, while for centerpiece stood a splendid entire meringue with MISS BIANCA in pink icing. The Prisoners' Aid Society brass band played Handel's *Water Music.*

It was the most beautiful picnic imaginable — especially because as so rarely happens at picnics everyone got a good sleep after lunch. What with all the exercise, and all the fresh air, and all the food, even the youngsters curled up practically with their mouths full. One particularly happy result was that no one made speeches.

Then the refreshed brass band struck up anew, now launching into the livelier strains of jigs and schottisches. Sets were formed and partners taken — and how the lily leaf rocked at last! — not to any watery ripple, but to the stamp and patter of dancing feet!

They danced The Dashing Brown Mouse, and Roll Out the Walnuts, and Jenny's Whiskers; then they danced Hickory-Dickory, and Mousetown Races, and that oldest favorite of all, Belling the Cat!

Bernard and Miss Bianca sat a little apart under the shade of an unfolding bud. Miss Bianca had of course opened the ball with him, but though lily pads make the most wonderful dance floors, being so exceptionally well sprung, she was rather easily tired. (Her own choice, in preference to The Dashing Brown Mouse, would have been that charming minuet Le Camembert; but she was too thoughtful to ask for it, lest no one else knew the steps.) In any case, she altogether preferred to sit and admire the view.

"What an exquisite scene!" murmured Miss Bianca. "Do observe, Bernard, the reflection of the turret in the moat! It's quite like Canaletto!"

"It's a bit in need of repair," said Bernard.

"Which makes it but the more picturesque!" pointed out Miss Bianca.

They were both right. Though its top part was now no more than a wig of ivy tods, the turret commanding the moat even in dilapidation still rose slender and colorful. It was built of yellow marble, which where unconcealed by ivy gleamed softly in the now declining sun. The ivy grew thicker as it climbed: until about three-fourths of the way up but empaneled, between

twin stems thick as the trunk of an old vine, a long honey-colored shaft; in which, near the top, a single window still solidly barred provided the necessary dark accent . . .

"Exquisite indeed!" repeated Miss Bianca. — "But what, I wonder," she added, "can be that bit of white up there?"

Bernard followed her glance. There was indeed something white fluttering just above the windowsill.

"Probably a piece of paper," said Bernard, "or a paper napkin. I dare say some people who picnic here leave their litter to blow about."

"How shocking!" exclaimed Miss Bianca. Amongst the several other offices she was discarding was that of President of the Mouse Anti-Litter League; but old habit remained strong, and indeed Miss Bianca was anti-litter by nature. "Especially in such picturesque surroundings as these!" exclaimed Miss Bianca indignantly. "Bernard, do send someone to fetch it down!"

A Boy Scout paddling by on a twig seemed only too glad of the errand. So indeed seemed several more Boy Scouts: before you could say Baden-Powell half-a-dozen were scrambling up the ivy, and after some slight endeavor they returned to lay their trophy in Miss Bianca's lap. — It proved to be not paper after all, but linen, a long shred like a hem. "*Really!*" cried Miss Bianca. "To throw away paper napkins is bad enough, but to discard *linen* ones argues complete irresponsibility! — Now, don't throw it back in the moat, Bernard; keep it till you see a bin."

At that moment the brass band struck up the mouse National Anthem.* All stood to attention, especially Bernard. It was time for Miss Bianca to return thanks; she rose, supported on Bernard's arm, and gracefully bowed. — She was additionally supported, of course, by the knowledge that she was looking her best: thanks to the lacy handkerchief not a hair was out of place. It also gave her rather the air of a court lady of the time of Louis the Fifteenth; and if half the mice present couldn't have told one Louis from the next, all instinctively applauded her aristocratic charm.

"Dear friends," began Miss Bianca, as soon as she could make herself heard, "pray believe that I do not exaggerate when I tell you this has been the happiest day of my life. I only hope it has been enjoyable to you too — "

"You bet it has!" cried one of the young dancers — who had actually got engaged to the mouse of his dreams halfway through Hickory-Dickory.

"So I see," smiled Miss Bianca, "by the set of your whiskers! You must invite me to the wedding! — But

---

* "Mice of the World, Unite." This is the solemn andante part. The chorus, allegretto, goes: "Cheese, cheese, beautiful cheese."

I hope we older, soberer folk have enjoyed this delightful excursion almost as much."

"Hear, hear!" cried all the mice.

"So that this picnic you have been good enough to arrange for me," continued Miss Bianca, "may ever remain as happy a memory to you all as it will to your grateful ex–Madam Chairwoman. Regretfully indeed I retire to private life — but warmed to the heart by your kindness!"

"Hear, hear!" cried all the mice again. Actually, some of the more conservative were rather glad Miss Bianca was retiring to private life. The Mouse Prisoners' Aid Society as a body were all for cheering prisoners in their cells — mouse-duty from time immemorial: Miss Bianca's revolutionary ideas of getting prisoners *out* was something else, and the adventures she'd led the Ladies' Guild into, for example, with this aim, many husbands still reprobated. Thus male voices in particular swelled the cheering, as Miss Bianca made her final bow and once more on Bernard's arm stepped lightly into a canoe to regain land and the returning mail van.

"It really has been a happy day!" sighed Miss Bianca gratefully. "Dear Bernard, I hope you have enjoyed it too?"

"Every minute," said Bernard sincerely. "Especially

as it means the end of your risking your life amongst jailers and bloodhounds."

"Of course you are quite right," agreed Miss Bianca. "I know myself that my nerves have become over-strained . . . What a happy day indeed!"

She cast a last backward glance, as the mail van moved off, towards the now deserted scene of revelry. Darkling lay the lily moat, yet still as beautiful as at noon; tall and slender rose the turret against the sun-set —

With, above its windowsill, *a second scrap of white replacing the first!*

2

All the way home Miss Bianca sat rather silent and preoccupied; but since most of the other mice were rather silent too, after their day's pleasuring, it wasn't remarked. Only Bernard glanced anxiously at her from time to time, and escorted her back to the Porcelain Pagoda with even more than his usual solicitude.

"Tomorrow I hope you'll take things very easily," said Bernard, as Miss Bianca untied the lace handkerchief from about her head and sank gratefully upon the chaise longue. "Let me get you a glass of milk."

"Thank you, no," said Miss Bianca, still in a preoccupied sort of way. "Bernard: that turret above the moat —"

"If you didn't like my calling it dilapidated, I'm sorry," said Bernard. "It's more like a Canaletto than any turret I've ever seen."

"Is that *all* you saw?" asked Miss Bianca.

"Well, yes," apologized Bernard. "You know I'm not very strong on Art . . ."

"This is not a question of Art, but of fact," said Miss Bianca gravely. "Bernard: I tell you that that turret above the moat *has a prisoner in it!*"

3

Bernard jumped. Then he smiled an indulgent smile.

"So that's what's been bothering you," he said. "Well, at least you haven't caught cold! Though why you should imagine any such thing —"

"I didn't imagine," interrupted Miss Bianca, "I *observed. I* observed, if you did not, a second signal fluttering at the window! — For so I am now convinced the first to have been; also no doubt *tied* to the bars (rather than blown against them) by some imprisoned hand within. Let me look!"

Reluctantly, with growing uneasiness, Bernard pulled the linen shred from his mackintosh pocket.

Before handing it over he took a quick look himself:
quite plainly (and how unfortunately!) one end indeed showed the creases of a knot.

"I dare say some other picnic party tied it there, just
for sport," he suggested. "Remember how our Scouts
enjoyed the climb?"

But Miss Bianca was too busy examining the trophy
even to consider this reasonable hypothesis.

"I was wrong," she murmured. "It isn't the hem of
a napkin, it is the hem of a handkerchief. And with a
name on it . . ."

" 'J. Fromage,' perhaps?" suggested Bernard, with a
desperate attempt at facetiousness. But never was facetiousness iller-timed.

"No; not J. Fromage," said Miss Bianca quietly,
"Mandrake."

4

Bernard seized the scrap from her shaking hands;
there, sure enough, the hateful name was still faintly
visible.

"So he's got his deserts at last!" said Bernard grimly.

Miss Bianca nodded.

"One can see how it happened. The Grand Duchess
would be angered to the last degree by his allowing the
child to escape . . ."

23

"I dare say the turret belongs to her," agreed Bernard. "She owns all sorts of places she's let go to rack and ruin. — To think of Mandrake up there under the leads," said Bernard, with relish, "boiling in summer and freezing in winter, and probably starving all the year round! Well, at least no one's going to rescue *him!*"

To his astonishment Miss Bianca, whom he had naturally expected to share in his rejoicing, turned pale. — No doubt from shock, thought Bernard, or from the painful memories aroused; and added en-

24

couragingly that Mandrake was probably in leg-irons
as well.

"I only fear so," said Miss Bianca gravely.

"You only *fear* — ?" began Bernard, astonished
again; and paused, as an incredible suspicion dawned.
"You don't — you can't — mean you think *Mandrake*
ought to be rescued?"

"Indeed I do," said Miss Bianca.

5

"Of course he was completely odious," admitted
Miss Bianca, some minutes later. (Bernard now pacing
up and down as he always paced when thoroughly
upset; as he'd paced until he wore a track in his postage-
stamp carpet, Miss Bianca captive in the Duchess's
palace.) "In fact, Mandrake was the most odious person it has ever been my lot to encounter —"

"Crueler than the Head Jailer," Bernard reminded
her.

"There is nothing bad one can't say against him,"
admitted Miss Bianca. "He was the Grand Duchess's
jackal —"

"Without a single kindly word for a poor defenseless
orphan," reminded Bernard, tramping on.

"Exactly," said Miss Bianca. "You must know I
hold no brief for him —"

"You held him in abhorrence," reminded Bernard.

"I still do," said Miss Bianca. "But confined as he is, what chance has he of reform?"

Bernard suspended his tramping to look at her. She appeared certainly rather fatigued, but in no way feverish . . .

"Let's get this straight," said Bernard, speaking very carefully. "You mean that *Mandrake* should be *rescued* in order to give him a chance to *reform?*"

"Well, he can hardly reform in a turret," pointed out Miss Bianca. "Who could?"

"What makes you," persisted Bernard, still very carefully, "think that he *would* reform? Have you any *grounds* for thinking he would?"

"No," said Miss Bianca simply. "I only hope."

For once Bernard lost all patience with her.

"Tell that to the Prisoners' Aid Society!" he exploded.

"Which is precisely," said Miss Bianca, "what I propose to do."

3

At the Moot-hall

THE NEXT MEETING in the Moot-hall took place some three days later. Miss Bianca had meant to attend in any case, since not to do so, at the inauguration of a new Madam Chairwoman, would have seemed discourteous; and the very fact that she didn't much care for her successor (a very tough games-mistress mouse, in Miss Bianca's opinion far too fond of giving orders) made her all the more punctilious. She had intended to sit as unobtrusively as possible, and certainly without speaking!

"But in such circumstances as these," thought Miss Bianca, "I shall really *have* to speak; for Bernard won't, and how else is Mandrake's case to be put forward? For once, any refinement of good manners must go by the board."

She still tried to *enter* the Moot-hall unobtrusively — arriving, indeed, so early, it was only a quarter full. An usher who attempted to lead her to a front matchbox she politely but firmly ignored, and sat down about the middle. To have sat down absolutely at the *back*, amongst the scuffling hobbledehoys eating popcorn, would have been conspicuous: Miss Bianca with her usual tact chose a place in just the right row (say about M), next to a short-sighted chemist. — He wasn't eating popcorn, but sucking lozenges, and politely offered one without recognizing her. Miss Bianca of course accepted it, though with but a smile; only the stone-deaf could have failed to recognize her *voice!* The flavor was perfectly innocuous, also there was a wrapping of silver paper, out of which she made a cocked hat while the Hall filled up. When upon her other side sat down a timid housewife who just said "Oh, my!" and relapsed into awestruck silence, Miss Bianca began to feel quite comfortable.

It still cost her a slight pang to see Bernard lead the new Madam Chairwoman out upon the platform. Miss Bianca had resigned of her own free will and didn't regret it; but there must ever be a sadness in seeing oneself supplanted. She stood up and applauded with the rest, however, and actually led a supplementary round, after Bernard's brief speech of introduction.

Then the new Madam Chairwoman made a speech. Her style was very different from Miss Bianca's: in curt, gruff tones she almost snapped out her thanks to the Society and Secretary for their confidence in her;

and was almost shouting, as she went on to adjure
more general attention to physical fitness. (All incom-
ing Chairwomen choose a special theme for their in-
augural address. Miss Bianca's had been The Quality
of Mercy.) As for *appearance*, Miss Bianca with the
best will in the world couldn't help being critical: a
pride in one's calling is entirely proper — but was it
really necessary, wasn't it rather derogatory to the dignity of the Society, to appear on the platform in a
gym slip?

However, all the mice seemed quite satisfied. ("The
charm of novelty!" thought Miss Bianca wryly.) Some
even sat up straighter on their matchboxes, under the
games-mistress's harangue. It nonetheless went on far
too long, and as the hobbledehoys at the back began
to shuffle their feet about, Bernard seized the opportunity of a pause between two breaths to make a con-
clusion.

"Three cheers and thank you very much," inter-
posed Bernard, stumping forward again. "I'm sure our
new Madam Chairwoman's words will be taken to
heart by one and all; now, since there is nothing on
the Agenda save our welcome to her I propose the
Meeting adjourns to supper. Any seconder?"

Half the front row shot up their hands. In another
moment the meeting would have been over — which
was exactly what Bernard intended. *He* had seen Miss

Bianca in row M, and hoped by this means to prevent her from courting a rebuff. But even as he reached for the Minute Book, Miss Bianca rose.

2

To do so required a considerable effort. Courtesy alone enjoined silence; also after having been given such a splendid picnic, any immediate further claim on the Society's notice smacked of a prima donna's post-farewell, positively-last-until-the-next reappearance. It was a true sacrifice Miss Bianca made, of elegance to altruism, as she rose and spoke.

"On a point of order," called Miss Bianca clearly, "may one raise from the floor a subject *not* on the Agenda?"

At once, at the sound of that famous silvery voice, every neck craned. Murmurings of "Look who!" and "She's here!" were heard on all sides.

"Well, I'm not sure —" began Bernard.

"Jolly well *out* of order, *I* should say," snapped the games-mistress.

But the mice applauded Miss Bianca so vigorously, there was no doubt of their wish to hear her, and even Bernard was so nettled by the games-mistress's tone, he made no attempt to overrule them but resigned himself to the inevitable.

"Thank you," said Miss Bianca. "Further to praise

our new Madam Chairwoman," she continued, "is obviously superfluous; but would it not be a happy thought to mark her inauguration, as it were with a white stone, by some distinctively heroic enterprise on the part of the Society as a whole?"

"Yes, yes!" "Go on!" "Tell how!" cried all the mice. Miss Bianca let them wait a moment.

"How little did we think," she began again, "dancing on the lily pads — on the occasion of that memorable picnic you were so kind as to offer me — that within the very turret that overlooked our revels, a prisoner still languished! How our gaiety must have mocked his ears! But such is the case; and what a glorious issue if, as a result, freedom should once more blossom for him like a splendid water lily!"

It must be admitted that half the members of the Society always listened to Miss Bianca simply spellbound by her beautiful delivery and exquisite choice of words. It was a sort of mass hypnotism, from which they awoke finding themselves committed to all sorts of surprising projects. But in this instance the magic had barely begun to work before the games-mistress, from the platform, broke in.

"Suggestion noted," barked the games-mistress. "Secretary, put it in the Minutes! — Can the speaker give any *particulars* of this prisoner? — such as his *name*, for instance?"

Far too soon, Miss Bianca had to.

"Mandrake," said Miss Bianca bravely. "His name is Mandrake . . ."

3

There fell a deathly silence. Every mouse in the Hall knew of Mandrake and how wicked he was. Ironically enough, it was Miss Bianca's own heroism, in rescuing an orphan from his and the Grand Duchess's clutches, that had made him so widely ill-famed! — Until now mothers scared bad children to obedience by the threat that Mandrake was coming for them . . .

Out of the silence rose a hiss.

Miss Bianca had never in her life been hissed before. For once she had to pause for words; her whiskers quivered. If only she'd been on the platform! How much easier, *from the platform,* Miss Bianca now realized, to sway the emotions of a Meeting! Quite a number of members couldn't even see her. But she had a place on the platform no longer, and in the moment while she paused to gather her resources the new Madam Chairwoman (having literally the upper hand) spoke again.

"The speaker's enthusiasm," she said loudly, "is I'm sure jolly creditable to her soft heart. I dare say a lot of *us* have soft hearts ourselves; but it needn't mean having soft heads! — Anyway, I'll put it to the vote: all those in favor of rescuing the notorious criminal Mandrake, hands up!"

Not a hand was raised.

"Motion put," snapped the games-mistress, "no seconder, rejected nem. con.!"

4

"I knew how it would be," said Bernard sympathetically, as he walked back with Miss Bianca to the Porcelain Pagoda. (He should already have been heading the supper table, but he saw she wanted to get home, and couldn't bear to let her leave the Moot-hall alone.) "I knew you'd get no help from the Society."

"Nor from you either?" sighed Miss Bianca. "Not even from you, Bernard?"

"Nor from me neither," returned Bernard, reluctantly but doggedly. "Though our new Madam Chairwoman might have been more tactful, I'm bound to say I agree with her: to set Mandrake at liberty would be to loose a monster on the world. You have made a most gallant, if in my opinion misguided, attempt to interest the Society on his behalf; it has failed; so do, please, Miss Bianca, just forget him and give all your attention to your nerves, also to that slim volume of verse so eagerly awaited."

Miss Bianca sighed again. Then, very delicately, she shrugged her ermine shoulders.

"Thank you, dear Bernard," she said, "for your excellent advice. — Now surely they're waiting for you to serve the soup?"

With an unhappy look, off Bernard stumped; Miss Bianca entered the Pagoda. It was the first time they had ever parted so coolly.

POEM BY MISS BIANCA,
WRITTEN THAT SAME NIGHT

Alone in gloom the wretched prisoner writhes,
Paying at last for all of evil done!
Yet is not Mercy still the strongest power
To bring him back, repentant, to the sun?

M. B.

She wrote another:

Alone the criminal? Lone too the hand
Outstretched to rehabilitate and free!
No friend to aid — the heavy task unshared
By e'en the Prisoners' Aid Society!

M. B.

This was the first time Miss Bianca had ever been able to work the Prisoners' Aid Society into a poem, so she was naturally rather pleased. Even so, it was with a heavy heart and troubled mind that she at last sought repose between her pink silk sheets.

4

A Daring Adventure

BUT THOUGH Miss Bianca no longer had the backing of the Society, though even Bernard refused his aid, anyone who thinks she was going to abandon her project of rescuing Mandrake will be mistaken. However fragile her nerves, beneath Miss Bianca's ermine coat beat a heart of truest steel — compared with which combination an iron hand in a velvet glove is but peanuts.

Bernard, if not the new Madam Chairwoman, had nonetheless succeeded in raising several doubts in her mind. How *could* she be sure Mandrake would reform? Had she *grounds* even for hope? What if the ex-steward emerged from captivity wickeder than ever — a monster loosed upon the world indeed? The longer Miss Bianca considered these awkward questions, the more clearly she perceived it her duty to obtain reliable (and satisfactory) answers to them, before taking independent action.

Obviously the only person competent to supply such answers was Mandrake himself.

"We must have a good long talk together!" thought Miss Bianca next morning.

But how to reach him?

"The Scouts climbed the ivy," thought Miss Bianca daringly, "why should not I ?"

She enjoyed at this time unusual freedom of movement, because the Boy was having his tonsils out. Naturally Miss Bianca had accompanied him to the nursing home — and would gladly have remained with him; only the Matron, as absolute in goodness as the Duchess in badness, refused to let her. "Poor Miss Bianca!" said the Boy's mother kindly, as they drove home together. "I'm afraid you're going to be dreadfully lonely, all by yourself in your Porcelain Pagoda!"

Of course Miss Bianca *was* lonely. On the other hand, without the Boy's lessons to superintend, and his playtime to share, she had unusual freedom of movement. Moreover, the Boy's tutor had been given a holiday, and his mother, now that the Boy wasn't there, no longer paid her regular suppertime visit to the schoolroom. Thus nobody noticed when that evening Miss Bianca wasn't there either!

She had actually caught the last outgoing mail van at seven. (She knew from experience that it was always easier to contact a prisoner at night; and coming home from the picnic, while seemingly so preoccupied, had in fact committed to memory the whole of the timetable pinned up in the driver's cab.) Since the journey back would be at about midnight, she took with her a light wrap and a morsel of cream cheese.

It was rather a pleasant trip, through the darkling fields beyond the city; although now less tootful than silent, the driver being a trifle weary and disinclined for exuberance. He was also disinclined to make unnecessary speed; long before the turret above the lily moat came into view Miss Bianca had shared her provision with a homing field mouse — the simplicity of whose manners quite excused his appetite. "Come any time convenient, ma'am, and sup your fill with me and my missus!" urged the field mouse, gratefully licking his whiskers. "Just don't tell she what I lost amongst the thimble-riggers at the fair!" Miss Bianca smilingly accepted the invitation for some future date; dropped off at last at the letterbox by the park gate, made her way to the moat, and there blandished the first water rat she encountered into sculling her across to the turret's foot. "I shan't be very long!" promised Miss Bianca. "Why, didn't I see 'ee but last week, dancing the prettiest of all?" coughed the water rat. (All water rats are by occupation subject to bronchitis.) "Rely on I waiting so long as you care, ma'am!"

Pleased by this humble tribute, and with no jailerish sounds to dismay, Miss Bianca attacked the ivy quite gaily. It proved a less difficult ascent than she had feared, the main stems were so thick and the leaves so steady. To slip between the window bars presented no difficulty at all: within ten minutes from landing there stood Miss Bianca at the prisoner's side!

2

Mandrake it was indeed; though Miss Bianca hardly recognized him.

In the Diamond Palace, Mandrake, for all his wickedness, had always been clean and well shaven; dressed indeed rather richly — his close black tunic diamond-buttoned, his steward's chain diamond-studded, even a cast-off pair of the Duchess's diamond buckles ornamenting his shoes. What an alteration was now! Naturally the Grand Duchess, casting him into disfavor, had stripped him of every jewel: the lack of the buttons was the most obvious; without them Mandrake had been forced to hold his tunic together with lacings of ivy pushed through the holes on one side and on the other through the very cloth. His unbuckled shoes were similarly secured; while as though in pathetic remembrance of his old high office, a garland of withered ivy drooped about his neck . . .

But even these changes were as nothing compared

with the change wrought by the mat of long gray hair tangling first with his bushy eyebrows, then with a long gray beard. His face was scarcely visible; only the jutting beak of his nose identified him. Altogether, as he crouched upon an untidy pallet-bed, he looked far less like Mandrake the Duchess's cruel steward, than like some poor old hermit of the woods; or like a broken old tree hung with Spanish moss.

Mandrake for his part didn't recognize Miss Bianca at all. How should he? The child in the Diamond Palace had always kept her safe out of his way in an apron pocket.

"Let me introduce myself," said Miss Bianca gently. "I am Miss Bianca."

To her horror, Mandrake cringed. — There had been a time when she would have rejoiced to see him cringe; but not now. Now, before such a poor old man of the woods, Miss Bianca felt nothing but compassion.

"Sent by Her Grace?" whimpered Mandrake. "Of course, obviously sent by Her Grace! — otherwise how would you come to be here? Present Her Grace my humble duty," whimpered Mandrake, "even if she has but sent you, as I suspect, to eat up any little bit of food I was saving for my supper!"

His clawlike hands absolutely clasped to his breast — tried to conceal beneath his beard — a rough bowl half-emptied of some sort of disgusting porridge. Miss

Bianca was forced to close her eyes a moment; but as soon as she had recovered from the slight attack of nausea, mounted lightly beside him on the pallet.

"My good Mandrake," she said soothingly, "pray credit me when I assure you that I have come neither upon the bidding of the Grand Duchess, nor to share your interestingly frugal meal. Have you by any chance heard of the Mouse Prisoners' Aid Society?"

The reason Miss Bianca brought in the Society, which of course wished no part of Mandrake at all, was because she felt a diffidence about seeming to take too much on her own shoulders, as unbecoming to feminine modesty. In fact the reference proved a lucky one; Mandrake's expression, very slightly, brightened.

"The Mouse Prisoners' Aid?" he repeated wonderingly. "Long ago, when I was out in the world, I indeed heard such a Society spoken of, amongst ticket-of-leave men." (What circles he must have frequented, thought Miss Bianca!) "Aye, and a good work it did," continued Mandrake, "cheering and befriending the unfortunate! Can it really be that you are come to cheer and befriend poor Mandrake?"

Touched to pity as she was, Miss Bianca remembered the object of her visit.

"That depends," said she, rather sternly. "Also pray do not refer to yourself in the third person, as though you were Julius Caesar. 'Unfortunate' is a description

43

most wrongdoers apply to themselves: you, Mandrake, I fear have been *bad*. Your long service with the Grand Duchess is in itself a certificate of badness."

"I had no option!" pleaded Mandrake, beginning to whimper again.

"Quite so," said Miss Bianca. "Some crime committed in early youth — the details of which, believe me, I would rather not know — put you in her power. Had you but paid the penalty at the time, you would not now — at least I hope not — find yourself confined and starving within a ruined turret."

"From which I may never, never regain liberty!" groaned Mandrake.

"That depends again," said Miss Bianca. "How would you employ yourself, if you regained liberty?"

She gazed earnestly into his face — or what she could see of it, through the tangle of gray hair. Very much hung upon his answer: upon whether it spoke a mind truly repentant, or still corrupt!

There was a long silence.

"Would you return, for instance, if it were possible, to Her Grace's service?" asked Miss Bianca.

"Never!" groaned Mandrake.

"Then what *would* you do?" pressed Miss Bianca.

"Well, if I could, I'd go as gardener to an orphanage," said Mandrake.

3

Miss Bianca was so surprised, as well as pleased, by this unexpected yet promising reply, it was with but an eloquent glance of approbation that she encouraged him to proceed.

"You are right," continued Mandrake, "in saying that I have been bad; I've been bad all my life, but never badder than while in Her Grace's service I allowed how many a defenseless orphan to pine away, without a word, which I might so easily have spoken, of kindness! Though the last actually achieved escape — not that you can know anything of *that* —"

(Miss Bianca forebore to enlighten him!)

"— and though it was that very escape that brought about my undoing, the tears of her predecessors haunt me still. If ever I had my liberty again," sighed Mandrake, "and if any orphanage would receive me (without pay, just my keep), I'd make its garden the prettiest, and the fruitfullest, and the best to be played in, any orphanage ever knew!"

Again there was a silence — but briefer, more poignant — while with his long gray beard he wiped away the tears now streaming down his face. Miss Bianca herself was not dry-eyed: a shake of her whiskers sent as it were one last diamond to jewel the ex-steward's ivy chain.

"Say no more, Mandrake!" cried Miss Bianca. "You shall be not only cheered, and befriended: you shall be *rescued!*"

Mandrake flinched.

4

There was no doubt about it; he flinched. Instead of meeting her enthusiastic gaze, he looked away. Miss Bianca hoped that he was but temporarily overcome by joy; in the circumstance, it would have been quite natural! But his next words, uttered, or rather mumbled, in a low, despairing tone, showed that such was not the case.

"It's very kind of you indeed," mumbled Mandrake. "Very kind I'm sure . . . but considering Her Grace's extraordinary powers, perhaps it would be best to leave me where I am."

"What!" exclaimed Miss Bianca.

"You can see for yourself," said Mandrake — in tones which really should have been *more* despairing — "there's no *way* of rescuing me. These walls of solid marble admit neither ingress nor exit; while even could the ivy bear my weight, which it cannot, the window's too small for me to get out of. There's no *hope* of rescuing me."

"Then why did you tie a signal to the bars?" demanded Miss Bianca.

"Well, it gave me something to do," explained Mandrake. "But I never thought anything would come of it . . ."

Miss Bianca perceived that though the dream of becoming a gardener in an orphanage was undoubtedly very precious to him — had possibly saved his reason, as he mentally set seedlings, pruned an orchard, rolled a tennis court — when it came to translating that dream into reality, with all the hazards necessary to be faced before it *could* be so translated, Mandrake to put it mildly was unprepared for heroism.

For a moment she felt nothing but indignant contempt. Then she looked at his porridge bowl.

"My poor Mandrake," said Miss Bianca, "I see you have allowed yourself to lapse into complete melancholia; which is indeed not to be wondered at; you are sadly undernourished. Of course there must be some means of *ingress* at least! — or how could you receive any food at all?"

"I don't know," sighed Mandrake. "It just comes."

"But that is nonsense," argued Miss Bianca. "Food cannot just come — unless in the form of a rabbit from a hat, or an apple falling from a tree: in either case uncooked. That porridge you hold *has* been cooked, however badly; someone must have *brought* it to you."

"Then I have never seen them," said Mandrake. "I fall asleep at night, my bowl empty; when I wake in the morning, it is filled. In my opinion, it's by the Duchess's black magic."

Miss Bianca was really annoyed. If there was one thing she didn't believe in, it was magic. She was too rational and well balanced. Certainly she didn't believe in porridge materializing out of thin air!

"Mandrake," said Miss Bianca firmly, "tonight you must keep awake!"

"I can't," groaned Mandrake. "In the beginning, I tried to; but I never could. I suppose that's another of Her Grace's spells."

"Nonsense," said Miss Bianca bracingly. "It is because, I repeat, you are undernourished. '*Qui dort, dîne*,' as they say in France! You must make one more effort."

"I'll try if you insist," sighed Mandrake. "But it won't be any use."

With growing concern Miss Bianca perceived that it wouldn't. Mandrake was beginning to nod already. The porridge bowl dropped from his hand and rolled away as flatter and flatter every moment Mandrake's gaunt, listless frame subsided on the pallet. Deplorable Mandrake! — incapable even of hope, equally incapable of self-help! Yet Miss Bianca did not abandon the potential gardener.

"There is nothing else to be done," thought Miss Bianca, "but that I should stay, and keep awake, myself!"

5

Consequences

FORTUNATELY IT IS quite easy for mice to keep awake at night. Night is the time when they by nature feel most active and alert. Miss Bianca took no credit to herself for her watchfulness; and not much for staying at all. Below a faithful water rat awaited, and if she didn't get back on the mail van she could always catch an early-morning milk cart. But she did wish Mandrake wouldn't snore so!

As the wind rose without and whistled through the ivy, each separate shrilling note was echoed by a positive blast from the ex-steward's hairy nostrils. Miss Bianca clasped her hands over her ears; then hastily dropped them again, fearful of missing some slight important sound. To occupy and distract herself she made a careful examination of each encircling wall. "For there *must*," argued Miss Bianca, "be *some* mode of entry! If only I knew more of architecture!"

But architecture was not yet among the Boy's studies, and Miss Bianca had never thought to take it up independently. Indeed, with all her other social and cultural activities, she could hardly have found time.

So as the night wore on, she just wrote a poem.

POEM BY MISS BIANCA,
WRITTEN IN MANDRAKE'S TURRET

Mandrake! Thou name once dreaded, now more meet
  For scornful pity, than for righteous rage!
How shall I ever get thee on thy feet,
  To lead to some receptive orphanage?

M. B.

She had barely completed the last line when the justice of her earlier speculations was dramatically confirmed by the sudden sliding into two parts of what had seemed a solid wall . . .

2

They slid apart, the two great marble slabs, so silently, Miss Bianca perceived at once why Mandrake never woke. — She still didn't suspect magic; she just appreciated the work of some very clever architect. Both the Grand Duchess and her late father the Grand Duke Tiberius had been known to employ the cleverest architects available, before beheading them.

51

Nor as the dwarfish bowlegged figure, carrying an iron pan, crept through, did Miss Bianca quail as at anything unearthly. In fact she recognized immediately one of the Duchess's criminal grooms. (Everyone in the Grand Duchess's household had been a criminal of some sort.) As he approached Mandrake's fallen bowl, he grinned. Grinning — and without even wiping it out first — he tipped in a new supply of porridge; and as swiftly and silently withdrew.

But not too swiftly for Miss Bianca! In the instant before the slabs kissed again — her tail actually brushing between — Miss Bianca had followed. There was no time to observe what machinery, what clever contrivance of weight and counterweight, operated; she could only follow — down a narrow circular staircase built within the thickness of the turret wall — down and down until at last she and her unwitting guide emerged together in a small malodorous apartment at ground level.

Probably it had once been the guard-room, when the turret formed part of a legitimate defensive stronghold. Now it looked more like a doss-house. Dirty blankets cumbered a floor otherwhere littered with empty tins, despite the summer heat a charcoal-burning brazier threw off fuggy fumes; while upon an old horsehair sofa with the stuffing coming out lolled a figure of definitely trampish, non-military aspect.

Miss Bianca recognized this figure also, as the second of the Grand Duchess's grooms.

"Duty done, George?" he yawned.

"Aye, duty done," grinned his comrade. "Thy turn tomorrow, Jack!"

"Which I must say will be a pleasure," grunted Jack. "Her Grace never put me upon a duty I liked more! — Were the tea leaves in, George?"

"Aye, and our nail-parings!" grinned George.

Miss Bianca shuddered. Even though she knew how harshly Mandrake had been used to treat the Duchess's grooms, she shuddered!

" 'Tis a marvel how the old chap holds out so long," mused George.

"The longer the better!" growled Jack. "The longer he lingers in misery won't thee and I be longer paid in idleness? 'Tis not as if he'd any chance of escape, that we need lose our sleep!"

"*So you think!*" cried Miss Bianca to herself. "*So you think!*"

But there was obviously nothing to be done at the moment, and the dreadfully stuffy atmosphere was beginning to make her feel quite faint. Fortunately she hadn't to climb down the ivy again to get away, she just slipped under the doorsill — and directly outside discovered in fact a narrow causeway linking the turret to the nearest shore. "My poor water rat!" thought Miss

54

Bianca remorsefully. "How long have I kept you un-necessarily from your bed!" But she still felt so con-fident of his faithfulness, she ran swiftly round the tur-ret's base, and there indeed he was. "Pray forgive me!" apologized Miss Bianca. "I was unexpectedly de-tained!"

The mail van had passed hours before, but she suc-cessfully caught an early-morning milk cart, and was back in the Porcelain Pagoda before a footman brought her breakfast — no one having noticed her absence.

Except Bernard.

3

Bernard arrived while she was still sipping coffee. His peal at the gate was so violent (before he discov-ered that the footman had carelessly left it open), Miss Bianca fully expected to see the bell-pull in his hand.

"My dear Bernard!" she exclaimed, smiling. "Is the Moot-hall on fire?"

"No, it isn't!" shouted Bernard.

"Then good morning," said Miss Bianca. "May I offer you a cup of coffee?"

"Good morning! No thank you!" cried Bernard. "Miss Bianca, where *were* you?"

"When?" asked Miss Bianca innocently.

"Last night," said Bernard more moderately, and mopping his brow with his handkerchief. "I called just about one o'clock: when you didn't answer the bell I thought perhaps there was some banquet going on, so I waited. I waited," accused Bernard, "until a quarter to three."

"You must surely know," objected Miss Bianca, "that diplomatic banquets always break up ere midnight? My dear Bernard, did you think I was at a *stag party?*"

— Before his obvious distress, however, she put badinage aside. Indeed his concern touched her particularly, after the coolness of their last parting; Miss Bianca truly valued Bernard, and was only too happy to be on good terms with him again. At the same time, her very regard impelled her to conceal from him an activity which she knew he would disapprove, and which would worry him as well. So she just said she was very sorry, she had been not at home.

This was rather disingenuous of Miss Bianca. — The phrase "not at home" is disingenuous in itself; it means one *is* at home but doesn't want to be bothered by callers. On the other hand, convention has made it perfectly acceptable. So Miss Bianca was really misleading Bernard into comfortableness when she let him think she actually *had* been at home, in the Porcelain Pagoda, when the facts were far otherwise.

"If you went to bed early, I only hope my ringing didn't disturb you," apologized Bernard, looking relieved.

"I never heard it," said Miss Bianca — again rather misleadingly. "Now do let me give you that cup of coffee!"

But Bernard, much as he wanted to stay, had to hurry off to keep an appointment, and Miss Bianca, much as she appreciated his concern, was glad to see him go, for she had a great deal to think about.

4

It is difficult enough to rescue a prisoner in any case; but far more difficult still when the prisoner doesn't want to be rescued.

"Alas, poor Mandrake!" thought Miss Bianca. "Alas, poor cowardly but still repentant Mandrake! What *is* to be done about him?"

She curled up upon the chaise longue and meditated.

"Obviously he has been undernourished for years," reflected Miss Bianca. "It is not to be wondered that his whole system, nervous as well as physical, has completely collapsed. Therefore the first step, equally obviously, must be to build him up again to robustness and courage by means of a balanced diet."

This was entirely sensible. But there were still difficulties — such as how to introduce a balanced diet into a ruined turret heavily guarded.

"Perhaps a course of vitamin pills would do?" thought Miss Bianca.

Pills were small enough to be sent through the post. But she very much doubted whether his jailers allowed Mandrake to receive mail. What if George and Jack *intercepted* the pills — even ate them up themselves — and so became stronger and wickeder than ever? Nor did there seem any possibility of bribery — Mandrake in captivity as good as a pension to them!

"Still, they do not keep particularly good watch," thought Miss Bianca. "Neither observed Mandrake's signal at the window: that they did not observe me either, climbing the ivy, is perhaps understandable, for it was dark, and I trod with great precaution; but no more did they observe, by broad daylight, a whole troop of Scouts climbing up!"

The reflection brought not only comfort, it brought an idea. Miss Bianca was too tired to examine it thoroughly at the moment, but at least it enabled her to sink into a long, deep, much-needed sleep.

6

The Scouts

DURING THE DAYS that followed any curious observer might have found Miss Bianca taking a rather unusual interest in the Prisoners' Aid Society Boy Scout troop. — Actually every mouse in town *was* a curious observer, Miss Bianca being such a public figure; however, most just considered it very nice of her that upon relinquishing the proud position of Madam Chairwoman, she allowed her benevolent attentions to be so humbly engaged.

Only their mothers thought much of the Prisoners' Aid Society Scouts. They were rather a ragtag outfit and numbered but six all told.

It was easy to see how this had come about: a first excellent Scoutmaster emigrated, a second, fatally, encountered a weasel; a third just resigned — but hadn't been replaced, because on every Agenda at the Moothall the item "Scouts" always came last, when there usually wasn't even a quorum to decide what should be done. Only a young half-Irish mouse named Shaun held the troop together at all.

Miss Bianca not only reviewed the Scouts before church on Sunday — the first Church Parade they'd put on for months; she not only visited their down-at-heel headquarters in an old oilcan, and gave prizes for table tennis; she actually invited Shaun to tea in her Porcelain Pagoda. It caused quite a sensation. Not that Shaun himself (half-Irish as he was) appeared abashed. His half-grown whiskers shone with brilliantine, he was curry-combed all over, his mother had spent half the morning replacing all the badges on his armlet by clean new ones — with the addition of two or three he wasn't strictly entitled to wear, if only because there was no one to examine him for Proficiency. Altogether Shaun felt himself a very handsome boy-o indeed, and an ornament even to the famous Miss Bianca's famous dwelling!

Miss Bianca, sensibly perceiving that the first thing necessary was to cut him down to size, at once pressed upon him a slice of toast so thickly spread with patum peperium as to bring tears to his eyes. After a couple more slices (which his pride forbade him to refuse), young Shaun sat looking much more respectful.

"What a great many badges you have!" observed Miss Bianca. "One for Trap Recognition, I see, and actually *two* for Cat Evasion!" (Shaun wished his mother had been more careful; but he really was proficient at Cat-Evading.) "And another for Cross-Country Running!" continued Miss Bianca, who had of course made herself mistress of the whole system. "Dear me, with such an accomplished leader, why is it, I wonder, that the Society's troop is so little in evidence?"

"The Society's not interested in us, ma'am," replied Shaun, "that's the reason. Why, 'twas only upon the occasion of your ladyship's grand picnic we've been let participate in anything at all."

"But how useful you were then," said Miss Bianca kindly, "tidying up the turret above the lily moat!"

"Ah, think nothing of it, ma'am," said Shaun. "The lads enjoyed it uncommonly, as an Exercise. Would we could get more such! — but now here's the entire summer holiday near gone by, without so much as a night under canvas."

"A week still remains," said Miss Bianca thoughtfully. "Though it does not involve actual camping out, would your troop care to make the climb again, do you suppose?"

"Would they not!" said Shaun.

"*Regularly?*" pressed Miss Bianca. "Say every day, for a week?"

"For a month!" declared Shaun.

"A month must be out of the question," said Miss

Bianca, "for you will all be back at school; but if for just a week your cooperation is available, the next thing to do is to swear you to secrecy."

2

There is nothing in all the world a Scout loves better — and particularly a half-Irish Scout — than to be sworn to secrecy. Shaun's eyes glowed with dedicated fire. His half-grown whiskers quivered with enthusiasm. He swore himself to secrecy three times over. — Miss Bianca could hardly *stop* him swearing himself to secrecy, in order to explain her project. Then in few but well-chosen words she laid the matter before him.

Her plan was that the entire troop, each member with a vitamin tablet in his knapsack, should daily ascend the turret to build Mandrake up. Miss Bianca didn't think six tablets a day at all too many, considering the ex-steward's sad condition; also the company and regular visiting (as showing her interest no mere flash in the pan) she trusted would raise his spirits as the vitamins toned his system. At the end of a week, with *forty-two* tablets inside him, and probably a Campfire song on his lips, Mandrake should be ready to make a bid for freedom!

Actually, she said nothing to Shaun about the bid-for-freedom part, for it would almost certainly involve risks which when she thought of their mothers Miss Bianca was determined no Scout should run. She presented the matter simply as a junior branch of welfare work.

Even this was enough to delight Shaun. Here was an Exercise at last! — and Miss Bianca's reiterated warning that the Society was to be kept in ignorance of it delighted him even more.

"For they'd never let us Scouts participate at all," gloated Shaun, "if they knew!"

"I assure you the only reason why they *shouldn't* know," said Miss Bianca hastily, "is because this *particular* case of welfare work would overburden an already full program, and so cause fruitless mental distress." (As ex-Chairwoman she had to be loyal to the Society — and from old friendship to Bernard its Secretary.) "Otherwise, your gallant services, I know, would be a source of extreme pride."

"Ah, tell that to your granny!" said Shaun easily. "Wasn't I there at the Meeting? All our new Madam Chairwoman's interested in is the old one-two-three!"

Miss Bianca's heart quite warmed to him. If she could have wished for more true altruism — for more true compassion as regarded Mandrake — at least she had found an enthusiasm to match her own. All that was necessary was to keep it within bounds.

"You must on no account be away from home all day," said Miss Bianca, "during the last week of vacation. Take the mail van that leaves at two (after dinner), then catch the four-forty back, and you may all be home in time for tea. Moreover there is no need to hire boats; on the further side of the turret you will find a causeway; pray keep off the water altogether!"

Shaun promised that her instructions should be followed to the dot, and went off whistling like a stormcock.

3

Miss Bianca supplied the vitamin tablets from the medicine chest in the Ambassador's bathroom: his

wife, the Boy's mother, had so often complained that
the Ambassador practically lived on them, Miss Bianca
felt no scruple about half-emptying four or five small
bottles. Some were for the nerves, others for the blood,
others again for General Lassitude; all quite peculiarly
apt, thought Miss Bianca, for the building up of Mandrake!

It was an interesting scene indeed, as she distrib-
uted the first issue to the Prisoners' Aid Society Boy
Scout troop assembled in their dilapidated oilcan.
Shaun, with his instinct for stage management, made
a proper ceremony of it: each Scout in turn stepped up
to Miss Bianca (standing on a cotton-reel), saluted,
shook hands, received his tablet, and saluted again.
Then all buckled their tablets into their knapsacks,
and Shaun led Miss Bianca round to inspect them. The
Scouts enjoyed every moment.

"Now three cheers for her ladyship!" cried Shaun.

"Hip, hip, hooray!" shouted all the troop — making
a quite respectable volume of sound, considering that
none of their voices had broken. — Their coats, too,
were still half-woolly; Miss Bianca, surveying them,
felt a momentary qualm. But it was only a run up the
ivy she asked of them, which they had achieved once
already without accident . . .

"Thank you," said Miss Bianca gracefully, "not only
for your kindness to myself, but also for your generous

66

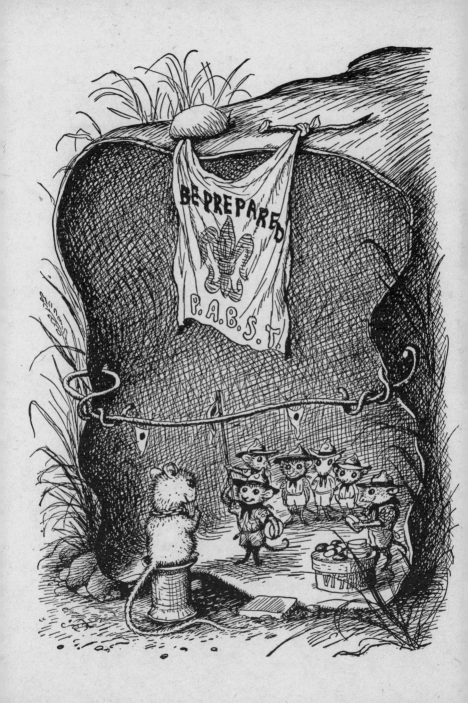

endeavors in a cause so near to every mouse's heart.
— Shaun," she added, in an undertone, "mind they
are all back for tea! You'd better come to the Pagoda
and report."

Then all the Scouts cheered again and marched off
in Indian file.

4

Miss Bianca herself did not spend the afternoon
idly. There is little point in rescuing a prisoner if when
at liberty he has nothing proper to do and nowhere
proper to go: Mandrake's ambition of turning orphanage gardener was on both counts quite ideal, but all
the more essential was it therefore to find some such
establishment willing to accept his services. There was
only one orphanage Miss Bianca could lay her hand
on — a large bleak building in the center of the city,
but with at least two acres of grounds. Thither she
made her way; and was soon in conversation with a respectable mole.

"What a very charming orchard!" exclaimed Miss
Bianca. (They met beneath a Granny Smith.) "But
are not the trees — forgive me if I show my ignorance!
— a little in need of *pruning?*"

"Aye," said the old mole. "In need of pruning they
be indeed!"

Miss Bianca strolled on towards a herbaceous border.

"And your perennials, what a blaze of color! — shouldn't some by now have been *cut down*," suggested Miss Bianca, "in preparation for the autumn?"

"So they should indeed!" said the old mole, trotting after her. He was greatly impressed by Miss Bianca's fur coat, which surpassed even his own.

"And a tennis court!" exclaimed Miss Bianca. "How delightfully situated, and what a pleasure, I'm sure, to

all your little guests! — But shouldn't it be *rolled*
more often?"

Here she was treading upon delicate ground indeed,
since to moles as a race even the Center Court at Wim-
bledon would be improved by a few neat molehills. But
this particular old mole had been so long connected
with an orphanage, he saw things quite from an orphan's point of view.

"Aye, so it should," he agreed. "Poor young critters,
sometimes the ball rises so unexpected-like, they give
'emselves black eyes wi' their own bats. Trouble is,
ma'am, we're shorthanded."

"Ah!" said Miss Bianca.

"Matron tells she can't afford a gardener not no-
how," grieved the mole, "wi' the price of e'en bare
bread so high. What *I* say is, what of all the apple jam
that could be got, were our trees but properly tended?"

"So that any conscientious gardener, *unpaid,* would
find a welcome here," suggested Miss Bianca, "whatever his background?"

"Lady, only find we such a one," said the mole earnestly, "and I'll warrant Matron content wi' no fore-
ground neither!"

"You encourage me extremely," said Miss Bianca.
"Pray forgive me for intruding upon your valuable
time."

7

Good and Bad

REALLY, EVERYTHING'S going quite beautifully!"
thought Miss Bianca.

Evening by evening Shaun arrived punctually at the
Porcelain Pagoda to report all members of the troop
safe home and having tea. ("I hope their mothers don't
miss them too much," asked Miss Bianca anxiously,
"away as they are all afternoon?" But Shaun said everyone's mother was looking a month younger.) He himself showed a disposition to linger, especially after
Miss Bianca, on the first occasion, rewarded him with
a slice of toast and patum peperium. (She in fact
offered toast and shrimp paste, but Shaun, who seemed
to regard the patum as a personal challenge, asked for
it particularly.) He also reported the prisoner Mandrake in increasingly good shape, and knocking back
vitamin pills like billy-o.

Miss Bianca was specially glad to hear this — even
so slangily expressed — because it had occurred to her
that Mandrake, in his pathologically suspicious state,

might have regarded the pills as poison sent by the Grand Duchess; but it appeared that Shaun's reference to the Prisoners' Aid Society had at once reassured. "The first couple went down a bit queasily," admitted Shaun, "but now Himself can't hardly wait, for the next issue!"

"And they are really doing him good?" pressed Miss Bianca.

"He's not the same man," Shaun assured her. "Why, if your ladyship could see him this minute, you'd take him for a proper Hercules!"

Even allowing for Irish exaggeration, if even half what Shaun said was true Miss Bianca really wondered whether she shouldn't write the pill-makers a testimonial!

Actually Shaun didn't report quite *everything* that happened, on the Exercise. He omitted, for instance, the hair-raising moment when the youngest member of the troop lost his footing on the ivy and plopped head-first into the lily moat. All the other Scouts enjoyed this incident extremely, it offered such a wonderful opportunity to practice first Lifesaving, then Artificial Respiration; each looked forward to two new badges for his armlet (awarded on the spot by Shaun). The young mouse was none the worse, though the vitamin pill in his knapsack dissolved and had to be reconstituted with chewing gum.

No more did Shaun report the equally hair-raising episode of the bat. It was he himself who encountered this uncanny creature, hanging upside down and sound asleep under the window ledge. Shaun had never seen a bat before, and the disconcerting physical resemblance to one of his own race, but *with wings,* so startled him, he almost followed his junior into the moat. — He slipped, he slid; only a particularly thick leaf cluster saved him — while the Scouts behind, alarmed at their leader's sudden declension, began to run back down the ivy in near panic. To avoid a complete débâcle Shaun had absolutely to awake and ask the bat to move — who, equally startled at seeing one apparently of *his* own race *without* wings, flittered off shrieking into the unaccustomed daylight. The entire troop thought they'd seen a ghost (as it were poor Aunt Maggie turned into an angel), and in the ensuing discussion Shaun accidentally blacked someone's eye . . .

In fact, there were several exciting episodes Shaun didn't report to Miss Bianca. But after whatever adventures the Scouts always got home to tea; and Mandrake punctually received his six tablets per day; so that everything really *was* going quite beautifully.

Which was more than could be said of the parent Society!

2

Not that under its new Madam Chairwoman the Mouse Prisoners' Aid Society had ceased to function — on the contrary. It was functioning more vigorously than ever: only not on traditional lines.

The games-mistress was so energetic, she called a General Meeting every single night; but then took all Minutes as Read, and gave short talks on physical culture, followed by exercises for each age group. Younger members touched their toes and vaulted, the elders

performed easy rhythmic movements; it was all very well thought-out and useful, but a decided change. Miss Bianca personally welcomed an excuse not to attend (she was already so slender and agile, no one expected it of her), but she felt very sorry for Bernard, who had to.

"Do you perform easy rhythmic movements too, Bernard?" she inquired curiously.

"No, I don't," growled Bernard. "We settled *that* in Committee."

"And in Committee, how do you get on with our new Madam Chairwoman?" asked Miss Bianca.

"Horribly," said Bernard. "She bosses everyone about."

" 'Tis an *esprit,* one must admit, *un peu fort,*" said Miss Bianca. "But then what energy, and dedication! Also you must remember that she was voted to the Chair quite unanimously, which naturally gives her confidence."

"Who else was there to vote for?" asked Bernard wearily. "When you wouldn't carry on (though don't for a moment think I wanted you to), who else was there? I can't remember when we've had such a poor lot of ladies — that is, in an executive sort of way. We wanted someone who could speak up and was used to running things — and by George we've got her!"

He directed a passing kick at a flowerpot. (This

particular conversation took place in the Pagoda grounds, the gate of which he happened to be strolling by when Miss Bianca came out to water her plants.)

"But what is worst of all," continued Bernard, "and setting aside all personal discomfort, is that she's diverting the Society from its true aims. We're not to cheer and befriend prisoners any more, let alone rescue 'em; we're just to take a millimeter off our waists!"

Miss Bianca listened with growing concern. Whatever her own criticisms of her successor (and though she couldn't help feeling a *little* pleased that Bernard now evidently shared them), the interests of the Society lay ever close to her heart. It had been amongst the most famous branches of the whole international organization — one of its decorations ranking above both the Jean Fromage Medal and the Tybalt Star for Gallantry in Face of Cats. The thought of its now declining to a mere gymnastic course was painful indeed.

"The promotion of physical fitness," said Miss Bianca, after a moment's pause, during which she tied up a daisy, "is of course entirely admirable; but surely there must be *some* captive on the Agenda?"

(She phrased the question as discreetly as possible, in case Bernard should think she was bringing up Mandrake again. But Bernard, originally reassured by her silence on the subject, and then what with all his other troubles, had in fact forgotten Mandrake's existence.)

77

"If you mean, isn't the Society keeping an eye on the Police files," said he, "I'm afraid the answer's no. I don't know whether you recall the name of our contact there — "

"Tubby Embonpoint," supplied Miss Bianca.

"Exactly," said Bernard. "Our new Madam Chairwoman can't stand the sight of him. Every report poor old Tubby brings in she simply won't let him stay to read — and then as soon as he's gone just tears up. I can see you think me pusillanimous," added Bernard unhappily, "for not making a flaming row about it; but with attendances falling off as they are, I feel that a united front on the platform must at all costs be preserved."

"There is that, certainly," said Miss Bianca.

"So I suppose I must just soldier on," said Bernard, with a sigh, "and hold things together as best I can until her term of office ends next year . . ."

3

"One, two, three and touch your toes!" shouted the games-mistress. "All in front swing right, swing left!"

The by now diminished assembly in the Moot-hall more or less obeyed. At the back there was a good deal of horseplay; in front several of the more elderly mice just sat down. Bernard, who on the platform had been sitting down all the time, continued sedentary. "Good-ness me!" shouted the games-mistress. "What a slack lot you all are! Now let's try the one-two-three again!"

The response was so poor, however, even she saw it was time to break up. After their first enthusiasm the mice were already tired of being bullied; in the jostle at the exit more than one was heard to mutter some-thing about this being *the last time,* while others mut-tered things like *"Never again unless there's nothing on the telly,"* or *"Not unless your sisters drop in . . ."*

So the Meeting broke up. Bernard only hoped and prayed that the whole Mouse Prisoners' Aid Society wasn't breaking up too!

8

The Plan

BY CONTRAST, as has been seen, everything in Miss Bianca's own private maverick branch was going quite beautifully; yet oddly enough it was for this very reason that she began to lose sleep again.

Looking ahead to the actual *rescue* of Mandrake, she perceived the time almost ripe. The ex-steward had indeed been built up far more swiftly than she anticipated; and she had found future employment for him so easily! Truth to tell, Miss Bianca was caught unprepared, and had as yet no proper plan of rescue at all; and her pink silk pillows fell to the floor, and her pink silk sheets crumpled, as she tossed and turned trying to think of one.

"He cannot be got out through the window," thought Miss Bianca, "for besides being barred, it is too small; nor if he could is the ivy capable of bearing

his weight. There is of course the stairway, only I don't know how to work the machinery! Mandrake would need to be swift indeed, to slip between those two great blocks on the heels of George or Jack! — and even if he should succeed, would not George, or Jack, observe him, and immediately summon the aid of Jack, or George?"

However much Mandrake might have been built up on vitamins, neither George nor Jack had looked in *need* of building up; and they had the advantage of numbers.

"Really, one scarcely knows where to *begin!*" thought Miss Bianca.

Yet after too long a delay — the Scouts having ceased their ministrations and gone back to school — might not the effect of the vitamins *wear off*, and Mandrake sink back into General Lassitude?

Or supposing the orphanage found another gardener?

These were troubling thoughts indeed, and more than once Miss Bianca longed for Bernard's sensible advice and masculine support. But she was resolved to make no further attempt on his sympathies — not from pride, but because she recognized that from his own point of view (believing Mandrake such a monster) Bernard was right; and though fully aware of her power over him not for worlds would she have *wheedled* him into doing anything against his conscience. Besides being a perfect lady, Miss Bianca was also a perfect gentleman.

When Bernard anxiously remarked on her distrait air, she told him she was correcting proofs — always a very trying occupation.

"Your slim volume of verse?" said Bernard respectfully. "Put me down for six copies."

Actually Miss Bianca *was* preparing her poems for the press, but so preoccupied was she with the ex-steward's fate, even though the printers waited she kept breaking off to write new ones. Such as —

POEM WRITTEN BY MISS BIANCA WHEN SHE
OUGHT TO HAVE BEEN CORRECTING PROOFS

O Mandrake, on thy feet at last,
Shall I not call thee rather Hercules?
Employment waits, thy crimes are past,
Come forth to prune th' expectant shrubs and
trees,
Come forth to tend each sweet neglected flower!
— But how to free thee from thy horrid tower?
                                        M. B.

2

She was actually thus engaged when Shaun came to make his penultimate report. It was so identical with all those preceding — every Scout safe home, Mandrake in fine fettle — Miss Bianca really didn't pay much attention. Shaun's lingering rather irritated her. He'd wolfed down quite four slices of toast spread with patum, of which he could now swallow any amount without a choke, but even so he still lingered while Miss Bianca rustled her papers about with a preoccupied air.

"Only another two days before school," observed Shaun conversationally.

"Time flies indeed," agreed Miss Bianca — but rising from her desk to give him a hint.

Shaun didn't take it. From his now-customary position on the foot of the chaise longue he regarded her brightly.

" 'Twasn't so much that I was thinking of," said he. "What *I* was thinking of was, isn't it about time we set about planning the rescue?"

Miss Bianca's whiskers quivered with surprise. — Also with dismay: she had been so particularly careful to give the Scouts no hint of what their Exercise was really leading up to! It was far too dangerous! (Of course she didn't know about the Lifesaving or the bat, or she would have thought even the welfare part too dangerous.)

"My dear boy," exclaimed Miss Bianca, as lightly as she could, "whoever put such an idea as *that* into your head?"

"Why, Himself, of course," said Shaun. "Ever since he's been feeling a bit more lively he talks of nothing else but your ladyship's promise to rescue him . . ."

"Oh, dear!" thought Miss Bianca. "O foolish, irresponsible Mandrake, to babble so!" But upon a moment's reflection she saw the injustice of the charge: she hadn't *warned* Mandrake to keep his mouth shut.

84

"It is I who have been irresponsible!" Miss Bianca chided herself. Still, she couldn't deny her promise, for that would have made Mandrake out a liar.

"Indeed, rescued he is to be," she admitted cautiously. "But *your* part in the undertaking has already — and how gallantly! — been played, by supplying him with vitamin pills, without which he could never have found strength to cooperate. The actual rescue itself must be left to older heads."

"Then your ladyship won't be taking part either?" suggested Shaun — O the Irish flatterer!

"Naturally I shall," corrected Miss Bianca (though concealing a smile). "But whatever plan is adopted, you, I repeat, will have no share in it, nor any other Scout; so please don't bother me now."

Shaun sighed.

"No doubt your ladyship has a grand scheme already prepared?" he said respectfully. " 'Twould be a treat to hear it."

"I think you had perhaps better remain in ignorance," said Miss Bianca severely.

"Ah, come on!" cajoled Shaun. "Didn't we climb the ivy? And amn't I sworn to secrecy? Tell just the first step."

Miss Bianca hesitated. But he really deserved *some* reward, and his gaze was so very respectful, she felt she could easily satisfy him with a few generalities.

"Well, of course the *first* step," said Miss Bianca, "is to lead Mandrake forth from his turret-chamber . . ."

"By the stairway," supplied Shaun intelligently.

3

Miss Bianca sat down again. If she had been surprised and dismayed before, she was now even more so! — and really needed something behind her back.

"How can *you* know of the stairway?" she cried. "Coming back as you do on the four-forty van?"

"Isn't there another out at seven?" said Shaun. "I've been returning on my own several nights past, to see just what goes on. And as the window's too small, let alone being barred, the stair hasn't it got to be?"

"Exactly so," said Miss Bianca. "It was what I had decided upon myself. — I'm afraid you have far exceeded your instructions."

"Mine's an inquiring disposition," explained Shaun. " 'Tis a pity George, or Jack, carries that porridge up so late."

"What, have you encountered them also?" cried Miss Bianca. "The Duchess's criminal grooms?"

"I thought they'd been grooms," agreed Shaun. "Can't you always tell a groom, by the cut of his legs? A pair of rough tough boy-os they are too!"

"Which is all the more reason," said Miss Bianca —

striving to regain command of a conversation so unexpectedly developing — "why neither you nor any of the Scouts should have business with them. Suppose Mandrake indeed enabled to make his escape down the stairway at dead of night —"

"I'd say, better by day," interrupted Shaun. "I'll tell why later."

"— he would still find George, or Jack, on guard below," pointed out Miss Bianca, "and what could even the whole troop do, against such ruffians?"

"A couple of kicks might well make a mash of the lot of us," agreed Shaun. (Miss Bianca shuddered.) "Therefore their attention must by no means be attracted, at the crucial moment, but rather diverted. As to which," said Shaun, without false modesty, "I've a very fine scheme myself — if your ladyship would care to hear it."

Again Miss Bianca hesitated; though this time more briefly. Shaun was looking more conceited every minute, and he was quite conceited enough already; but at whatever damage to his character Miss Bianca, having still no clear idea herself how to set about rescuing Mandrake, couldn't afford not to listen to even a Boy Scout who *had*. She even sketched an inviting gesture towards the patum-pot. Shaun took a spoonful neat.

"Pray proceed," said Miss Bianca. "The distracting of George's and Jack's attention I agree highly desirable; I myself could easily get them seats to a Symphony Concert, or even to the Opera; but since I doubt whether they are musical, any suggestion, or opinion, you may contribute, will interest me extremely."

"Well, in my opinion," said Shaun, "the answer's horses."

4

"Horses?" repeated Miss Bianca blankly.

"Aren't they grooms?" explained Shaun. "What groom could ever resist the sight of a fine horse? A string of racehorses exercising in the park, what groom could resist nipping out to take a look? For an hour at least I'd warrant neither George nor Jack on duty — especially were Sir Hector in the lead!"

Miss Bianca listened with increasing attention. Though no race-goer, even she had heard of Sir Hector. He was the great national favorite, beloved by all for the regularity with which he brought small odds-on dividends to many a humble pocket. Even citizens who sensibly didn't bet at all turned out just to admire his majestic stride past the winning post. No jockey had ever pulled him; the only one who ever tried to Sir Hector contemptuously threw at the first fence — and then, such was his magnanimous nature, stood protectively above while the rest of the field thundered by.

"I should quite like to see Sir Hector myself," confessed Miss Bianca. "Also I begin to perceive why any hour of darkness is unsuitable."

"Six A.M. it must be at the earliest," said Shaun. "Sir Hector's never out exercising sooner. Any move on Himself's part in the meantime would attract attention for sure! — In my opinion, those great sliding slabs must be jammed apart overnight."

To Miss Bianca's eager but prudent inquiry *how,* Shaun at first easily replied, by the bodies of the entire troop, after which all could be buried together in one heroes' grave. But upon her pointing out how much this would distress their mothers he thought again, and suggested employing Mandrake's porridge bowl instead. Especially with a fresh supply of porridge spilling forth Shaun promised it fatal to any delicate machinery whatever; and he himself undertook to roll it instantly into place on the heels of Jack, or George.

"Neither of whom ever look back," gloated Shaun, "to see does the wall close or no. They're too confident altogether! As they gape after Sir Hector on the morrow, old Mandrake may stroll down the stair at gentlemanly ease!"

Miss Bianca was beginning to feel almost confident herself. She was still more experienced in prisoner-rescuing than Shaun.

"I don't know that I'd advise *strolling,*" said Miss

Bianca. "There is ever the slip between cup and lip; Mandrake must make all speed possible towards the park gate, where halts a city-bound milk cart."

"Trust your ladyship to look so far ahead!" said Shaun admiringly. "Without your ladyship I'm sure we'd get nowhere at all!"

Miss Bianca smiled. She knew she was being flattered; all the same, half her cares seemed lifted by Shaun's resourcefulness, as a proper plan took shape at last!

A doubt occurred nonetheless.

"Surely Sir Hector," she suggested, "does not usually exercise in public? Has he not — of course I know nothing about racing; one merely picks up a phrase! — his own private Gallops to exercise upon?"

For the first time Shaun hesitated.

"True enough," said he, "and very fine and private Gallops they are. — Just for this once, he'd have to be persuaded to make a change . . ."

"And who is to persuade him?" asked Miss Bianca nervously.

"Why, your ladyship, of course!" said Shaun.

5

Thus it was upon Miss Bianca's shoulders that rested the first, cardinal preliminary to Mandrake's rescue: that of inducing Sir Hector (whom she didn't even know by sight) to change the venue of his morning exercise from his own private Gallops to the parkland about the turret. Upon this all else depended.

"Oh, dear!" thought Miss Bianca. "I suppose I'd better call on him tomorrow!"

9

Sir Hector

THE BOY WAS still in his nursing home: no one noticed Miss Bianca's absence next morning, from the
Porcelain Pagoda, as in the back seat of an Attaché's
sports car she drove towards Sir Hector's famous establishment. (A taste for racing, on the part of his At-
tachés, the Ambassador rather frowned upon. Miss
Bianca, having herself made free with the Ambassador's vitamin pills, felt in no position to be censori-
ous.) The Attaché in question was actually lunching
at the stables — so she had plenty of time in which to
operate.

There was thus no occasion for flurry; but in fact
Miss Bianca did feel just a *little* flurried. For a single
lady to pay an uninvited call upon a perfectly strange
single gentleman was a complete breach of etiquette:
behavior not only unconventional, but almost bold;
and Miss Bianca habitually reserved her boldness for
such situations as fleeing from bloodhounds. Nor did

the first sight of Sir Hector's domain do anything to promote female confidence. All good racing stables are beautifully kept — posts and chains whitewashed, each stall immaculate — and this one was so particularly; wherever the eye rested, not a flake of paint scaled, not a single blade of grass (in the center patch) fell below or rose above the general accurate level; but more characteristic still was the air of peculiarly masculine peace that brooded over all. Miss Bianca felt as though she had intruded upon a very good Club — such as the Athenæum in London.

Cautiously she advanced through the silent, dinner-time-empty yard. Not an equine head showed, above the half-doors of the stalls; over each, however, was written the name of its occupant — Nutmeg, Galga, Coquette; Patches, Timotheus, Golden Boy — so that at least she was in no danger of calling on the wrong person, always a very awkward thing to do. Sir Hector's stall was the ultimate, superior in size to all the rest, and if possible more immaculately kept. The other names were painted in black on white, but Sir Hector's in letters of gold.

"I wonder what is the correct procedure?" thought Miss Bianca.

There was no bell, or knocker, with which to attract attention. She had of course a visiting card with her, but mouse-size visiting cards are so small, she feared that if she just slipped it under the door Sir Hector might not notice it — or he might even tread upon it. "Really, a person of such consequence should have a butler!" thought Miss Bianca quite crossly. — In fact, it was rare indeed for Sir Hector to be left so unattended, but all the common grooms were at their meal, and his own special groom had slipped out to visit a sick aunt. (With Sir Hector's leave: it was a mystery in the stables how explicitly the two communicated, but they did.) Miss Bianca was not aware of all this, so her censure was perhaps justified. But however in favor of the conventions, she wasn't bigoted about them, and however much she would have preferred to be properly announced, she had small hesitation in slipping her person, rather than her card, under the sill.

— For a moment, it seemed as though she emerged beneath a great golden waterfall. Crinkly and bright, silken-shiny and rustling, the glorious wave poured down and almost blinded her. — Was it a waterfall, or was it fireworks? — It was neither. It was Sir Hector's tail.

2

Nor did the rest of his person prove less breathtaking in handsomeness. Sir Hector stood seventeen hands high; beneath a skin soft as a lady's glove his splendid muscles rippled with easy virile power. His mane, unlike his free-flowing tail intricately plaited, lent a touch of dandyism that but enhanced this masculinity — like the knot of ribbons at a Cavalier's shoulder. His ancestral Arab blood showed in a short, strong, superbly flexing neck — swanlike for grace, bull-like in strength; while his eyes for topaz brilliance matched Miss Bianca's own!

For a moment Miss Bianca was quite overcome. Then, carefully skirting the most majestic forelegs imaginable, she ran lightly up upon Sir Hector's manger, and halted but an inch from his equally majestic nose.

"Pray pardon the intrusion," said she, a trifle breathlessly. "Also be assured that only on business of extreme urgency would I venture to disturb you. Let me introduce myself: I am Miss Bianca."

However much surprised, Sir Hector was far too well-bred to show it. Considering that he had just waked up from a sound sleep, his answering words displayed in fact not only his breeding, but also uncommon presence of mind.

"A lady I have long desired to meet," said Sir Hector courteously. "Miss Bianca's distinguished services to humanity have made her famous indeed!"

Miss Bianca, who never lost poise for more than a

moment, accepted the compliment with a modest bow.
— Anything else would have been hypocritical; she
knew she was famous, just as Sir Hector knew *he* was
famous; but by an accompanying smile and little shake
of the head she managed to imply that *he* was *more*
famous. If this sounds complicated, it was quite easy
to Miss Bianca, with her long training in diplomatic
circles, where volumes can be spoken by a raised Ambassadorial eyebrow.

As for Sir Hector, he was immediately reassured that
Miss Bianca hadn't come to ask for racing tips (as even
the finest ladies had been known to do) and added that
he much regretted not being able to offer her a proper
seat. Miss Bianca with equal politeness replied that she
always preferred to stand. "As I believe you do yourself?" said Miss Bianca. "Also I shall not detain you
long!" "The longer the better!" said Sir Hector.

Actually Miss Bianca already felt that she would like
to stay a very long time indeed. She felt there were all
sorts of things she and Sir Hector could talk about —
such as the *burden* of fame, and what to do when
people wanted one's autograph. (She could never dis-
cuss such problems with Bernard, because Bernard's
autograph was never wanted save on receipts for Prisoners' Aid Society dues. This was dreadfully unfair
to Bernard, who had been quite wonderfully heroic in
the Black Castle, for instance; the trouble was that he

lacked personality. Both Miss Bianca and Sir Hector had outstanding personalities.) But however enjoyable such a conversation, it wouldn't have been to the point; and Miss Bianca fully realized that she *was* disturbing Sir Hector's noontime repose. If he had a race that afternoon, how many humble wagers might not be put in hazard, through its lack! On the other hand, the topic of Mandrake did need a little leading up to; and in the slight pause that followed Sir Hector spoke again.

"My own family tree boasts a famous lady also," said he, "though but collaterally. Her name was — Rosinante."

"The coadjutator of Don Quixote?" supplied Miss Bianca swiftly.

"Perhaps you have seen her portrait?" said Sir Hector, with a smile. "Dear me, she'd hardly have won a Selling Plate! But it is the spirit that counts, even more than the bone; and it seems she had great magnanimity."

Miss Bianca siezed the opening.

"Which I am sure has been transmitted to every branch of the connection!" cried she. "You encourage me to be frank!"

And as briefly as possible she laid before him her whole plan.

3

Sir Hector listened with grave attention. Miss Bianca's task was in one way made easier because he already knew who the Grand Duchess was — a person whose wicked designs deserved thwarting whenever possible; less fortunately, he also knew who *Mandrake* was. As soon as he realized the object of Miss Bianca's benevolence, Sir Hector's brow darkened. Just like Bernard, he seemed positively to *approve* the ex-steward's incarceration! — and for all Miss Bianca's eloquence remained unmoved.

"My dear little lady," he pronounced at last, "you do not know, and I am happy to think it, the depths of human depravity. There is no more chance of Mandrake's true repentance than of my being beaten by a rank outsider."

"But he *has* repented!" protested Miss Bianca. "His ambition now is to become a gardener! Does not *that* show true repentance? — Did not Lord Bacon, the great English jurist, aver gardening the purest, the most *innocent*, of all human pleasures — or occupations?"

"If I remember my history," said Sir Hector, "Lord Bacon was no innocent himself. Much as it grieves me to disappoint you —"

"You disappoint me indeed!" cried Miss Bianca,

quite passionately. "As I am sure you would disappoint the Lady Rosinante also! She, I am convinced, would have heard my appeal with more sympathy!"

A small globule, like a dewdrop, rolled along one whisker and fell sparkling upon her silvery fur. — Miss Bianca hadn't meant to cry; if there was one argument she disdained to employ it was the unfair female argument of tears. She simply couldn't help herself; and immediately wiped her eyes with her tail. This can be a very graceful gesture, when elegantly performed, which was of course how Miss Bianca performed it, though quite unconsciously.

"Pray pardon my emotion," she apologized, with dignity. "My nerves are somewhat overwrought; I should

tell you that I am also in the middle of correcting proofs. Pray forgive me, too, for disturbing your repose. Perhaps one day I shall have the pleasure of seeing you on the racecourse; in which case, I assure you, I shall wear my very best hat!"

It wasn't Miss Bianca's tears that moved Sir Hector; it was her gallantry.

"If my mere presence, in the parkland —" he began thoughtfully.

Miss Bianca, in the act of descending from the manger, paused. Again quite unconsciously, just because all her movements were so graceful, she paused in a peculiarly charming attitude — one tiny foot advanced, the rest of her person sweetly balanced for the first jump. The connoisseur's eye of Sir Hector rested on her appreciatively.

"If my mere presence," he repeated, "without any further obligation —"

"But that is all I ask!" cried Miss Bianca joyfully. "Of course I wouldn't expect you to *speak* to Mandrake! And it is, isn't it, just a matter of a hint to your groom?"

"He will no doubt think me whimsical," smiled Sir Hector, "but perhaps I am entitled to a whim. Until tomorrow, then, upon the parkland!"

4

No one ever quite knew, in the stables, how the idea originated. It was just generally accepted that whatever Sir Hector's groom said, went. Sir Hector's groom himself (their communications being always wordless) didn't know exactly how the idea had been put into *his* mind. But Sir Hector having given him leave, also wordlessly, to visit a sick aunt, he loyally promoted the favorite's whim to exercise for once upon the parkland, instead of upon his own private Gallops; and of course Sir Hector's jockey had to agree.

POEM COMPOSED BY MISS BIANCA ON HER WAY BACK
IN THE ATTACHÉ'S SPORTS CAR

My beautiful, my beautiful! that standest meekly by,
With thy proudly arched and glossy neck, and dark and
fiery eye!

She had got just so far when she realized that this poem had been written already, by the Hon. Mrs. Norton. So she had to start again, and in fact achieved one of her very best.

Wind's flashing speed, great Ocean's force,
In one majestic frame combine!
But ah, the spirit is the Sun
That animates with life divine!

M. B.

10

To the Rescue!

SIR HECTOR'S cooperation thus assured, Miss Bianca and Shaun sat down together to prepare in detail the full plan for Mandrake's liberation.

— Shaun was waiting at the Pagoda to hear *Miss Bianca's* report; and she had by this time recognized the hopelessness of trying to keep him uninvolved. All the other Scouts, however, she insisted should play no part; and Shaun, as always brimming with self-confidence — and, it must be admitted, rather a hog for glory — entirely agreed.

"Now take a piece of paper, Shaun," directed Miss Bianca, "and write down *One*."

Step One was to climb the ivy to Mandrake's chamber in plenty of time to prepare his mind for his release. Also Miss Bianca — Step One-A — would take a pair of scissors with which to cut his hair.

"What about a shave?" suggested Shaun.

"Quite impossible," said Miss Bianca firmly. "But at

least by extensive clipping he can be made presentable at the gates of an orphanage."

Step Two was to instruct him to feign sleep, concealing his newly shorn head under the blanket, at the moment when George or Jack came up with the porridge. Then immediately the groom withdrew — Step Three — Shaun would swiftly roll Mandrake's bowl between the sliding marble slabs and jam them apart.

"Leave me alone for that!" promised Shaun. "Amn't I the best dribbler on the football team?"

Step Four was perhaps the most difficult of all, as comprising the period of waiting. — Miss Bianca thought they should all go to sleep, to recruit their energies, and suggested taking an alarm clock. Of course she didn't possess such a vulgar mechanism herself, but Shaun said he could easily borrow one, to be set for five-thirty.

That left half an hour — Step Five — in which to tidy up and watch for Sir Hector from the turret window. Then as soon as the latter had rounded the moat, thus coming into view of George and Jack below, rescued and rescuers alike would descend by the stairway to find, if all went well, the guard-room unguarded.

"As I'll lay any odds 'twill be," cried Shaun, "and the door swinging open! A sight of Sir Hector'd draw Jack and George from their graves, let alone from their duty! Step Six is easy as pie — and as for Step Seven, 'tis but old Mandrake's skating off to catch the milk cart!"

"Which we ourselves I trust may take also," said Miss Bianca, "and so be back in time for lunch. Now go home, my dear boy, make a good supper, be sure to borrow the alarm clock, and meet me at the G.P.O. at seven."

2

Shaun left. Miss Bianca ate a little cream cheese herself, and put her feet up on the chaise longue.

Even the whole Prisoners' Aid Society, she thought, couldn't have conceived any *better* plan for rescuing Mandrake!

Of course the Prisoners' Aid Society had refused to consider rescuing Mandrake at all.

So had Bernard refused.

"Oh, dear!" thought Miss Bianca. "I do hope I'm not making a mistake!"

Such doubts necessarily cross the minds of even those most dedicated to good causes, when it comes to the actual point of doing something others equally dedicated thoroughly disapprove of. (The Society, under its new leadership, possibly wasn't quite so dedicated as it used to be; but Bernard certainly was.)

"Also I have involved Sir Hector," thought Miss Bianca, "and if in any unworthy cause, how shall I ever forgive myself? O Mandrake, do *pray* show yourself worthy!"

None of these qualms, however, altered her resolution; having set her hand to the plow Miss Bianca was not one to turn back; but it was perhaps fortunate that she couldn't find her scissors. She was always losing them — and this time she had to hunt through her workbox and her bureau drawers, and look behind ornaments and feel down chairs — all she could find was a pair from her manicure set, with which she would really have to clip Mandrake one hair at a time! Miss Bianca was looking for her *big* scissors, and like many another lady couldn't remember where she'd put them. They came to light at last between the leaves of an illustrated volume on Byzantine Art. Miss Bianca was quite distressed, she was as a rule so respectful of books, and it just showed how worried she had been; but the search most usefully distracted her mind from further brooding, before she met Shaun at the G.P.O.

3

It was actually just as Shaun and Miss Bianca settled themselves comfortably among the mailbags that Bernard, most *un*comfortably, though in his own home, received a deputation from the Prisoners' Aid Society.

Bernard's home was a very nice bachelor flat in the

bottom drawer of an empty cigar cabinet. (Since the Ambassador gave up smoking, this was about the best address possible for a mouse; there were waiting lists inches long, and most of the other flats were occupied by doctors and bankers.) Bernard was rather proud of his cedarwood paneling and postage-stamp carpet, and as a rule welcomed visitors; but eight angry members crowding in at once promised less of social pleasure than of official embarrassment.

"Now, look here, Bernard — or rather, Mr. Secretary," began the spokesman (thus confirming Bernard's worst fears), "we've had about enough of it!"

Bernard, as he pulled up chairs, ran a hasty but experienced eye over the whole party. Four were old and stout, but four quite young; five were male, three female; altogether a very representative group . . .

"Of what?" he asked uneasily.

"Of being badgered about by our new Madam Chairwoman," said the spokesman. "That's what."

His seven companions uttered a low "Hear, hear." Bernard poured out bottled beer all round. Though every word, including the Hear-hears, found an echo in his own heart, he owed it to his office to uphold the dignity of the Chair.

"The lady to whom you refer," he said severely, "is undoubtedly a bit of a pill; but it was you yourselves who elected her, and as I remember, unanimously."

"In error," said the spokesman.

"Goodness me, you can't pretend you thought she was anyone different!" exclaimed Bernard.

"Maybe not; but we thought she'd *behave* differently," said the spokesman. "That is, differently from the way she's behaving now. — When have we ever before," demanded the spokesman, with rising indignation, "attended at the Moot-hall merely to receive *pep-talks?* — to be harangued into doing *exercises?* Quite apart from the fact that I like my wife's figure as it is —"

"Darling!" exclaimed the stouter of the ladies.

"— slimming is not the object, nor ever has been, nor ever should be, of our famous Society. What sort of example is being set the junior members? — one of whom I believe has a word to say on the subject himself? — Speak up, boy!"

Instantly one of the younger mice rose, consulted a piece of paper, closed his eyes and said all in one breath:

"On behalf of all junior members of the Prisoners' Aid Society I wish to state one and all distressed, disappointed and dislocated." Then he opened his eyes again and added, more colloquially, "Which means that if there's to be no more facing of jailers, or bearding of cats, or at least cheering of prisoners going on, us'll just switch to the Y.M.C.A."

He had scarcely sat down before up rose the spokes-man's wife in turn.

"As we members of the Ladies' Guild shall change our allegiance also," she stated, "to the Townswomen's Institute. What *we* have to say" (and here she too con-sulted a piece of paper) "is where is the point in pre-paring suppers if there can't be anything *nice?* Is Mr. Secretary aware that the new Madam Chairwoman has actually supplied us with a *calorie chart?*"

"And tape measures!" put in another lady.

"And dumbbells," added the spokesman grimly. "Well, Mr. Secretary, you see the situation. Voted into the Chair unanimously or not, unless her term of office is cut short I for one prophesy the complete disintegra-tion of our Society. What do you propose to do about it?"

Again poor Bernard agreed with every word. But he could only take refuge in the rules.

"A term of office can't be cut short," he pointed out. "A year's a year and there you are. Unless the incum-bent resigns or dies, she's in for a year."

"She won't resign," said the spokesman dourly. "She's too fond of giving orders."

"And she appears to enjoy uncommonly robust health," said Bernard. "Of course there *is* assassination, but I hardly suppose you'd recommend *that?*"

"In the interests of the Society I'm not sure that I

wouldn't," said the spokesman. "However, we leave it to you."

4

What a painful situation was Bernard's, left alone washing up the glasses! Of course he knew he wasn't really expected to assassinate the games-mistress; but undoubtedly *something* was expected of him, in the way of getting rid of her. Vain now were his hopes that he could hold the Society together by just soldiering on!

He had been prepared to. He had been prepared to stomach every rudeness of the new Madam Chairwoman in Committee, and then back her up on the platform, in the interests of the M.P.A.S. He was even prepared, if it came to the point, to swing a dumbbell himself. He knew he'd look pretty silly with a dumbbell, but he was prepared.

The heroism of people like Bernard isn't the showy sort. Other people often don't recognize it as heroism at all. But it is.

Only now that it seemed that just soldiering on wouldn't be enough, what else could he do? As Bernard thought and thought he became so agitated and upset, he cracked his best engraved goblet against the tap; and answered a knock at the door with still shaking hands.

It was Mrs. Spokesman, come back for her umbrella. Or that was why she said she'd come back, and there indeed it was, in the hall. But as Bernard politely pointed it out to her —

"Bernard," said she, in a low, meaningful voice.

"Well?" said Bernard.

She hesitated. Then she looked over his shoulder into the kitchen and saw the broken glass, and in a busybody sort of way bustled in before he could stop her, and began picking up the fragments as though *that* was what she'd come for . . .

"It wasn't my best," lied Bernard — like all men jealous of his prowess as a washer-up.

"At least let's hope not one of a set," said Mrs. Spokesman. "But my poor dear Bernard, how you need a wife!"

5

Bernard froze on his feet. It was as though some dreadful lurking notion at the back of his own mind had suddenly leaped out red in tooth and claw.

"It isn't the first time I've thought of it," continued Mrs. Spokesman kindly. "Of course we all appreciate your devotion to Miss Bianca — as indeed who isn't devoted to Miss Bianca? I'm sure all we members of the Ladies' Guild are! — even while appreciating *her* resolve to remain single. Only Jean Fromage (were he alive) could be an acceptable match! What *you* need is I will not say an *ordinary* wife, but certainly a wife who besides taking a keen interest in public affairs would also wash up your glasses for you!"

Bernard backed against the sink.

"I see you take my meaning," said Mrs. Spokesman, with an arch smile. "And I'm sure Someone Else would agree with me! Someone Else having such a very particular regard for you!"

Of course Bernard knew at once who she meant. She meant the games-mistress.

"I don't believe a word!" he cried desperately.

"It's true as I stand," said Mrs. Spokesman. "Haven't you noticed how often she calls a Committee?"

"Because she likes taking the Chair!" implored Bernard.

"Not at all; to enjoy the pleasure of Mr. Secretary's company," corrected the spokesman's wife, with another horribly arch smile. "We women know one another! Beneath that gym slip, in the opinion of the entire Ladies' Guild, beats a heart so overflowing with unrequited affection, once it *was* requited immediate resignation from all public duties would inevitably follow, as that Someone Else dedicated herself completely to a husband's interests. — Just think about it, Bernard."

With her umbrella in one hand and the broken glass wrapped up in newspaper in the other, the spokesman's wife then left. Bernard staggered into the sitting room and collapsed on the sofa. He felt dreadful.

Had he really no option but to marry the games-mistress, to save the Society from disruption? It looked like it.

"I suppose I could spend a good deal of time abroad, visiting other Branches," thought Bernard. *"Here,* I suppose, there'll be nothing but dumbbells all over the place and a calorie chart in the kitchen . . ."

He uttered such a groan, the sofa springs twanged in sympathy.

"And I suppose I could still go and see Miss Bianca," thought Bernard.

Painful as it had been to hear her resolve to remain single spoken of as an accepted fact, he himself (the point put so plainly) humbly acknowledged only the fabled Jean Fromage indeed worthy of her hand, and this in a way was a consolation, because Jean Fromage was dead. So long as Miss Bianca didn't marry *anyone,* Bernard felt he could be almost content with her affectionate friendship and the privilege of visiting at the Porcelain Pagoda whenever he liked.

Immediately, however, his main consolation was that at least she was out of it all — out of all squabbles and disagreeableness, let alone deadly perils. And since it was partly by his own influence that she had been led to retire (thus putting the whole Society in jeopardy, owing to the unexpectedly horrible character of her successor), he recognized the obligation to pay any price to keep the Society on the rails, lest she should start worrying over the consequences of her defection, to the detriment of her nerves.

Brave Bernard was steeled to every sacrifice by the picture of Miss Bianca in the peaceful security of the Porcelain Pagoda, tranquilly correcting proofs of her forthcoming slim volume of verse . . .

Who was in fact at that very moment engaged in cutting Mandrake's hair in the turret above the lily moat!

11

In the Turret

BEND YOUR HEAD a little to the left," said Miss Bianca. "What a pity it is you can't put your ears forward!"

Mandrake under her scissors sat passive — or rather subduing an impatience she was delighted to observe. Not a trace in him now appeared of General Lassitude; instead of cringing, he had seemed ready rather to chide her for delay; and instead of flinching before the prospect of being rescued, he showed positive impatience! There had been no need to prepare his mind at all; it was prepared already . . .

"I really must write those pill-makers a testimonial!" thought Miss Bianca, clipping away.

At least a foot of hair, at least a yard of beard she clipped off, while Shaun ran back and forth stuffing the fallen Spanish-moss-like tangles under the bed. Since she couldn't give Mandrake a shave she left him a neat Imperial; then she clipped his eyebrows; and when she had finished, Step One-A also was successfully achieved. Any orphanage in the world, thought Miss Bianca, would have welcomed Mandrake as gardener, such was his respectable and even distinguished appearance, especially unpaid!

Step Two equally succeeded. (One reason why Miss Bianca was so good at rescuing prisoners was because she never forgot the necessary order of Steps.) Mandrake, as instructed, lay down upon his pallet and was soon emitting such truly convincing snores Miss Bianca quite feared lest some of the pills had been for Insomnia. But by from time to time opening one eye he showed he was just entering into the spirit of the thing, and making the most of his temporarily passive part.

"Mind you set the alarm clock all the same!" said Miss Bianca to Shaun. "I do hope it's reliable!" — It had gone off three or four times in the mail van, though according to Shaun only because he was training it. As soon as it was set Miss Bianca took it away from him and into her own charge.

Step Three was the most exciting. As at about an hour after midnight the marble slabs slid apart; as, grim and grinning, one of the grooms (it happened to be George) stumped through with the porridge pan, and emptied it into Mandrake's bowl, and grinningly withdrew —

"Now!" breathed Miss Bianca.

In a flash Shaun was on the ball. — The best dribbler on the team, he shot Mandrake's bowl accurately between the closing stones. Though they shattered it, shards of earthenware mingling with porridge still jammed them apart. Nor did George look back. Too confident altogether stumped George down the stair — leaving the path to freedom open!

"Now for Step Four," said Miss Bianca coolly.

2

She had always known that Step Four would prove the most testing, and so indeed it did. Shaun, after she had taught him the first verse of Keats's Ode to Autumn (Miss Bianca never let slip a cultural opportunity), curled up and slept easily enough; Mandrake's histrionic snores were soon genuine; but Miss Bianca herself remained wakeful and a prey to nerves for hours and hours.

She had no reason to be nervous — or at any rate, not *quite* so nervous. Wasn't everything going really beautifully? — and her faith in Sir Hector absolute? As sure as the sun would rise, Sir Hector would keep his appointment; and when had any project failed to which he lent his countenance? Miss Bianca seemed to recall more than one County Show saved from utter disaster — rain falling in buckets, the ground a quag

— by his stately appearance, even under wraps. On the occasion when a race-course stand caught fire, his calm canter from the paddock to inspect the flames averted a panic and enabled him to win the National Cup with a full complement of spectators. In association with Sir Hector, how could any project fail?

Miss Bianca assured herself it couldn't.

— A sudden louder snore broke in upon her thoughts. She glanced towards the bed; and all at once the obscure source of her uneasiness became apparent.

The blanket now thrown aside, Mandrake's newly revealed profile jutted arrogantly forth — the nose like an eagle's beak, the thin cruel mouth that shut like a trap. Miss Bianca remembered it all too well, as that of the pitiless steward in the Diamond Palace. Asleep, Mandrake looked his old wicked self . . .

Miss Bianca trembled. "O Mandrake, do pray prove worthy!" she had implored — only a few hours ago, in her Porcelain Pagoda. With what earnestness did she now add the rider, "Or at least not thoroughly *un!*"

She was so agitated, she actually ran up upon the pallet and bent above his ear — intending to inject therein, for his subconscious to absorb while he slept, a few such phrases as "Meekness is all," "Pity the poor," and "Be not proud." But since she had felt a certain (very natural) repugnance about clipping the hair in Mandrake's ear-holes, she couldn't be sure her words penetrated; and upon descending, fell at last into a sleep almost as unrefreshing as wakefulness. She was glad indeed to hear the alarm go off at half-past five, to end such a restless, troubled night!

Luckier Shaun knew no such anxieties. He was up and spruced already, and out watching from the windowsill, as Miss Bianca first made her own hasty toilet, and then roused the now disturbing object of so much benevolent endeavor . . .

"Here they come," cried Shaun, "through the park gate — and Sir Hector leading!"

3

There is no prettier sight in the world than a string of racehorses out at exercise. The scrubbiest moorland or sandy track is adorned by their fleetness, and any natural beauty enhanced. The park about the ruined turret had long been considered by courting couples romantic; but not a butcher at odds with his wife could have failed to see it beautiful, as Sir Hector, followed by his five companions, paced forth upon its turf. The grass beneath their hooves took on a brighter green; trees about to shed their leaves saluted with a last flourish of rich foliage, as Sir Hector led in Galga, Coquette and Golden Boy, and Timotheus and Patches!

Miss Bianca, leaning over Shaun's shoulder, thought

of three poems at once. Shaun in his enthusiasm almost fell out and had to be pulled back by the tail. — Actually Miss Bianca leaned out nearly as far herself, in an attempt to catch Sir Hector's eye: the distance was too great, however, and racehorses rarely look up; but just a bird's-eye view of his glorious tail sufficed to raise her spirits. And that he had forgotten nothing of his promise was proved even as he rounded the moat and was lost to view: passing the ground-floor window of the guard-room, Sir Hector neighed so loudly, even had George and Jack been cooking breakfast, their attention must have been attracted.

Patches was the last to go by. (He always brought up the rear, being frankly too old for the work, and owing his place just to Sir Hector's kindly remembrance of past glories.) But though the excitement in the turret was by now intense, Miss Bianca restrained Shaun with one hand, and Mandrake with the other, until old Patches had vanished too, and only then gave proud Shaun the honor of first setting foot on the stair.

"Run down, Shaun, and see have George and Jack quitted the guard-room," she bade. "If not, stay until they do, then return and give word!"

But Shaun was down and up again in a trice.

"They're out both," he reported, "and the door just as didn't I tell you swinging open!"

"Then now for Step Six," said Miss Bianca (coolly).

4

Fortunately Mandrake was still so emaciated, even he could squeeze through the narrow gap. The stairway was steep and tortuous indeed, but with Shaun running before — and now, with the familiarity of an experienced guide, warning of a particularly high step or of one crumbled quite away — all gained the guardroom in safety. Empty it was indeed! — and the door swinging open! — so hastily had George and Jack run out!

Out ran Mandrake and Shaun and Miss Bianca too. Then they paused. It was still a moment for caution.

Sir Hector had by now cantered some quarter of a mile — in a direction opposite to the park gate where would halt the milk cart. Jack was panting after as fast as he could, every pant taking *him* farther from the park gate too; but George, the fatter and slower, waited still on the causeway's farther side to watch the rest of the string go by. Of course he wouldn't have noticed Shaun and Miss Bianca slipping behind him, but he would certainly have noticed Mandrake. "We must wait," breathed Miss Bianca, "until he too makes after!"

All three shrank back into the doorway. It seemed an age, while first Galga, then Coquette, then Timotheus and Golden Boy, cantered past; George seemed rooted to the spot. — Miss Bianca very much feared she heard Mandrake utter an unregenerate oath: the distressing thought that he might teach the orphans bad language for a moment, but unpleasantly, distracted her; she glanced up at him with a reproving, anxious look. Then she fixed her eyes again on George . . .

Would he *never* move? — or what if he moved in the wrong direction, *back,* to precipitate disaster?

But it was his own disaster George precipitated. Deceived by the long gap after Golden Boy, imagining the whole string gone by, with a whoop off he started in their wake — and straight into Patches's path!

On pounded old Patches, intent only upon following Sir Hector — contemptuous of his jockey's pull, too blind himself to see the need of swerving. George's back was turned; if Patches was half-blind, so did he seem half-deaf, as full in the path of those iron-shod hooves he lumbered forth! Another moment, and his criminal career would have been terminated for good in a mash of blood and bone —

Had he not been snatched to safety by whom but — Mandrake!

In a series of energetic leaps Mandrake bounded across the causeway and shouldered George to the ground, and rolled out of danger the last obstacle in his own path to freedom!

He had proved himself worthy indeed!

Shaun let out a cheer. As for Miss Bianca, she almost fainted with joyful emotion, to see her faith so justified. "O Mandrake, thou art even more reformed than I could hope!" she cried to herself. "O Mandrake, how could I ever doubt thee!"

— The next moment she almost fainted again. George, still upon the ground, as soon as he saw who his savior was, with the most appalling lack of gratitude seized Mandrake by the ankle, at the same time bawling out to Jack to come quick, their prisoner was escaping!

5

Mandrake wrenched himself free. "Oh, hurry!" cried Miss Bianca. "Hurry, towards the park gate!" "My ankle!" gasped Mandrake. It was sprained. He could but limp. Fortunately George, more severely incapacitated, couldn't rise from the ground at all. But Jack, in the distance, was already pounding towards them . . .

Shaun and Miss Bianca could run. (Shaun, it may be remembered, actually had a Badge for Cross-Country Running.) But how could they abandon the now crippled Mandrake to face even Jack alone? They couldn't. Yet what could they do when Jack caught up — as undoubtedly he would? Though the groom was

no greyhound, Mandrake could barely hobble. Nor could the mice support him; they were too short. One on either side they encouraged him to fresh efforts, they tried to encourage each other; but it was like a nightmare, to be forced to such slow progress in the face of such deadly peril!

"Look back, Shaun," whispered Miss Bianca. "Is Jack gaining on us very fast?"

"Fast enough," returned Shaun grimly.

"Then you at least must run," whispered Miss Bianca, "for your mother's sake!"

But Shaun suddenly said he was an orphan, and on they desperately, painfully labored.

Jack was no more than a hundred yards behind.

When he was but fifty yards behind, Mandrake stumbled; and all was lost.

12

The End

OR SO IT seemed.

At that very instant a glorious thunder of hooves shook the ground — Sir Hector was beside them! He had witnessed all — Mandrake's heroic act, George's base ingratitude, Jack's pursuit, and had covered half a mile in forty-nine seconds. His splendid eyes blazed with indignation, his saddle was empty; for the second time in his life, Sir Hector had spilled his jockey!

"Up on my back!" cried Sir Hector. "Up, all three!"

With a last astonishing effort Mandrake mounted. Shaun made a stirrup for Miss Bianca to reach Sir Hector's tail and himself swung up after. "Ready?" cried Sir Hector. "Aye!" responded Mandrake, in a loud, firm voice. — He was worth rescuing indeed! His ankle throbbed in agony, his hands on the reins were powerless, as Sir Hector began to canter it was all he could do to keep his seat, but not for a moment did his courage fail. "Carry me where you will," exclaimed Mandrake, through clenched teeth, "if need be to my death, but at least out of captivity!"

Miss Bianca quite palpitated with admiration — but nonetheless ran swiftly past the saddle to gain Sir Hector's ear.

"Not to his death, just to the Orphanage!" she begged.

"Sit close all the same," returned Sir Hector, breaking into a gallop. "For once, I'm going to show my paces!"

2

Like a whirlwind, like a sheet of flame over dry bracken, galloped Sir Hector through the parkland — a sight so glorious, the few early-morning pedestrians lucky enough to witness it never forgot it in all their lives. His tail streamed like a comet, the plaits of his mane like candle flames; from his nostrils (at least so one pedestrian asserted) flashed sparks of fire! Miss Bianca's silvery fur blew about like snowflakes; Shaun, even in the lee of the cantle, had to hold his whiskers on; Mandrake crouched ever lower and lower until he lay almost flat (thus accidentally offering the least wind resistance possible). Not only Jack was left far behind, but Sir Hector's stable-companions as well; though their dismayed jockeys took out the whip, Sir

Hector outdistanced them all with such contemptuous ease, when he at last entered the city it was at a walk.

"The Orphanage, I think you mentioned?" he inquired courteously of Miss Bianca. (He wasn't even out of breath.)

"If you would be so kind," said Miss Bianca. — She quite regretted that the ride was over. She adored speed, and clinging to Sir Hector's mane, had felt as safe as in the Ambassadorial car. But then one always *would* feel safe, thought Miss Bianca, with Sir Hector!

It seemed that their esteem was mutual. While Mandrake rang the Orphanage bell and waited for the door to open, the noble steed stooped his majestic head to Miss Bianca's level.

"By Pegasus, what an escapade you have led me into!" he said gently. "Mandrake's excellent conduct I admit fully justifies your faith in him; your feminine instinct was right; he *has* repented. But what *I* do not repent is having entered upon such an escapade solely for the sake of Miss Bianca!"

Miss Bianca blushed. Before she could reply — and indeed she would have found any reply difficult, such was her emotion — the Matron opened the Orphanage door. (The old mole had been quite right; they really were shorthanded.) Once again, how invaluable Sir Hector's aegis! The most respectable-looking gardener, without any references and asking no wages, might well have aroused suspicion; but seeing Mandrake as it were sponsored by the great national favorite, Matron engaged him at once.

"So now we part," said Sir Hector to Miss Bianca. "That is, unless I can drop you anywhere?"

Miss Bianca shook her head. After that wild and glorious ride, a mere *lift* would have been an anticlimax.

"Yet not, I trust, forever," said Sir Hector, smiling. "Perhaps one day you will visit me again; or even come to see me run, in your best hat? Though never, I suspect, better than you saw me run today!"

So low he stooped, his velvet nose brushed Miss Bianca's whiskers. But she braced herself for a final adieu. After all, Sir Hector stood seventeen hands high, and herself no more than two inches . . .

"Perhaps I shall prefer to keep a treasured memory," said Miss Bianca softly. "Today, was I not *up* with you?"

3

No medals were struck to commemorate this particular rescue, because it wasn't an official one — the Mouse Prisoners' Aid Society having played no part in it. Miss Bianca just invited all the Scouts to a splen-

did tea, and personally presented Shaun with an in-scribed wristwatch. It had luminous hands.

Nonetheless, since everything concerning Sir Hector was news, the details somehow got about, and the more they heard the more all members of the M.P.A.S. re-gretted that they *hadn't* played any part, to share the glory. As has been seen, it was mostly their own fault, in allowing the games-mistress to bully them out of generous enthusiasm into mere self-regarding physical culture; they still so shouted her down at the next Meeting, while she was explaining *why* no medals, even she saw the necessity to retire as fast as she could.

So Bernard hadn't to marry her after all; and was so glad that when no one else would subscribe for the usual presentation silver tea-tray he paid for it out of his own pocket. The new Madam Chairwoman elected in her place was a nice fat member of the Ladies' Guild, who proved quite as executive as needful. She was also a great admirer of Miss Bianca's, upon whose advice and inspiration she so relied, the future of the Society was in safe hands.

Mandrake as gardener to the Orphanage turned out a great success. He truly labored there day by day to make the orchard fruitful, so that apple jam flowed free, and the flowerbeds brilliant, and the tennis court playable upon. One of the orphans who played on it actually became Junior Champion, and was subsequently tapped for the Wightman Cup.

Miss Bianca's slim volume of verse went into three editions, after unanimously favorable reviews.

Her testimonial to the vitamin-pill makers was quoted throughout the popular press, and helped to save many a reader from General Lassitude.

The jockey spilled in the parkland Sir Hector had carefully spilled into a bracken-patch, and so received no injuries.

The mouse who got engaged at the picnic married his dream-mouse next week. Miss Bianca not only attended the wedding, but stood godmother to their first six children.

If Bernard was surprised to find her taking in all racing editions of all evening papers, he was just surprised. Miss Bianca never hurt his feelings by revealing what admiration had been aroused in her breast by Sir Hector's splendid appearance and heroic conduct. Bernard, on the other hand, blurted out all about having been prepared to marry the games-mistress; but since the ghastly sacrifice (as he forthrightly described it) had been envisaged solely in the interest of Miss Bianca's nerves, she was less jealous than touched. She ever treated him with all her old affection, and he spent most evenings at the Porcelain Pagoda.

There was even a new bond between them, since together they had saved the Prisoners' Aid Society from disaster — Miss Bianca by reminding it of the glory to be won by its proper work, Bernard by his gallant soldiering-on over an extraordinarily difficult period. Miss Bianca's contribution was the more exciting, Bernard's the more solidly practical; but each merited equal praise, and their joint achievement must ever be accounted a notable triumph by every thoughtful mouse.

THE END